Σvεαku Koppo

"What kind of
family draws
in an innocent
kid and makes
him the target
of murderers?"

NOWHERE TO RUN

UNSTOPPABLE

NOWHERE TO RUN

JUDE WATSON

SCHOLASTIC INC.

Library of Congress Control Number: 2013934701

ISBN 978-0-545-52137-6

10 9 8 7 6 5 4 3 2 1   13 14 15 16 17/0

Amy and Dan p. 28: Ken Karp for Scholastic; marble p. 36: CGTextures;
sign background p. 86: CGTextures; Amy and Dan p. 200: Ken Karp for Scholastic
Book design and illustration by Charice Silverman

First edition, October 2013

Printed in China 62

Scholastic US: 557 Broadway • New York, NY 10012
Scholastic Canada: 604 King Street West • Toronto, ON M5V 1E1
Scholastic New Zealand Limited: Private Bag 94407 • Greenmount, Manukau 2141
Scholastic UK Ltd.: Euston House • 24 Eversholt Street • London NW1 1DB

To the Katonah Village Library
for offering an armchair by the fireplace
and smiling librarians
even when I'm overdue.
— J.W.

PROLOGUE

Somewhere off the coast of Maine

There was only one house on the island. The rest was pine forest, a thick, dark, bristling screen that threw the beach into shadow for most of the sunlit summer days. It also concealed most of the buildings, the three pools — outdoor, indoor, and lap — the tennis courts, the helipad, the landing strip, and the four-car garage from any passing sailboat. Only tourists came close. The locals knew better.

They knew the muscled men in tight black T-shirts in the fast rubber boats who would cut your fishing line or blare a warning with a horn that could make your eardrums bleed.

They knew the treacherous currents, too. They knew how the wind seemed to whip through the channel at a speed and ferocity that you didn't feel in the harbor. They knew to stay away.

The sound of a violin soared through the still air. A sixteen-year-old girl watched her fingers moving without error, notes sliding and falling like pure water. What used to confound her now flowed. She knew that if she worked at her skill she could succeed, even though she had no talent.

That's what her father tells her.

The thirteen-year-old boy just defeated his tennis pro in straight sets without breaking a sweat. He saw the surprise on the pro's face. Just wait until the guy found out he was fired. The boy's dad always fires a coach after he's been defeated.

They lack the killer instinct, his father said. *You want to turn out like that?*

He whacked the tennis ball hard, sending it back over the net. The coach had bent down to retrieve his bag, and the ball slammed into his back. Ow. That must have *hurt*. The boy knew it well from experience.

"Never turn your back on a competitor!" the boy jeered.

That's what his father tells him.

Killer instinct.

Far out to sea, a man was swimming, moving as precisely and tirelessly as a machine. Even though he had three pools, he preferred swimming in the open sea. This year the seals had been swimming closer and closer to shore. This meant, he knew, that the great white sharks were lurking, moving constantly in order to feed.

It added a certain . . . spice to the swim.

The man reached the dock with several powerful

strokes. He hauled himself up and strode toward the house. A short but powerfully muscled man in a black T-shirt tossed him a towel, and he wiped his face and threw it on the ground. He did not worry about towels. They were picked up, laundered, and stacked again. He didn't have to see it or think about it. He was always thinking great thoughts now. Thoughts large and complex enough to take in the world.

He entered through the French doors into the den. He almost recoiled from the sight of hundreds of glassy eyes staring at him. His wife was arranging and rearranging her collection. Again. He hurried past before she had a chance to talk to him.

His office was cool and quiet. He pulled on a terry-cloth robe and activated the many transparent screens. Data flashed by, and he absorbed it all quickly and completely. Things were so different now. His strategic thinking was almost as fast as the computer data streaking across his screens.

Almost there. So close he could taste it.

There are only two people alive on the planet who can stop it.

It's time to eliminate them.

Somewhere near Mt. Washington, New Hampshire

In the small town where the men occasionally went for supplies, their story was that they were on a corporate retreat, testing their skills in the wilderness. The men—they were all men—looked remarkably alike. They were all fit and muscular with close-cropped hair. They usually wore track pants and T-shirts, or hiking gear. They were friendly, but not forthcoming. After they left, the shopkeeper or gas station attendant would realize that they were hard to tell apart. They had names that were hard to distinguish: Joe, Frank, John, Mike.

Over a hundred men had been shifted into and out of the camp, but for the past four weeks the group had been whittled down to six. Six of the best, six of the brightest, six of the most trustworthy.

They had always been in shape; that was their job. But this last month they'd doubled their strength and then doubled it again. They had climbed the mountain fourteen times. They attended classes in combat driving, surveillance, and martial arts. They had been fitted for Italian suits, handmade shoes with rubber soles, and jackets with pockets that will hold their weaponry close and without detection.

They were ready. They just didn't know for what.

All they knew was that they had never felt so powerful. So at the top of their game.

As they sat on hard chairs watching their screens flash with a simulated escape from a metropolitan area, the leader of the men heard the chime of a text. He was the tallest, and the tannest. His teeth were very white and even; his real teeth had been knocked out in a bar fight years ago in Corsica. His face registered no emotion as he told the rest that it was time to mobilize. They had received their targets.

He connected his phone to the computer. On a large transparent screen floated two photographs.

"Target One, Target Two," he said in a flat tone.

The men showed no emotion. Even though their targets were kids.

CHAPTER 1

Attleboro, Massachusetts

It was a sunny, beautiful day. A day you felt glad to be alive.

Too bad Amy Cahill was surrounded by the dead.

Amy bowed her head and squeezed her eyes shut. She was only sixteen, but she'd attended too many funerals. She'd said too many good-byes.

Six months ago she'd buried her cousin and her uncle, and today, a marker would be placed for William James McIntyre, family attorney and deeply loved friend.

Her cell phone chimed in her pocket. She slipped it out and read the text. It was from her boyfriend, Jake Rosenbloom. It was six hours later in Rome, where he lived. It would be close to dusk there, and he'd be putting away his books and starting to think about dinner.

I know the service is this morning. I wish I could be there with you. You ok?

Amy's finger was poised over the keyboard. Her gaze drifted down the grassy hill to where a polished gray marker stood gleaming next to weathered, tilting gravestones, the many generations of the Tolliver family who had lived in Attleboro since before the Revolutionary War. Too far away to read the name, but she didn't have to.

EVAN JOSEPH TOLLIVER

She slipped her phone back in her pocket. Tears stung her eyes. She'd put on a black dress and gone to Evan's wake six months earlier. His mother had shut the door in her face. Amy had understood. After all, she blamed herself for Evan's death just as much as his mother did. If it weren't for Amy, Evan would still be alive. He would still be volunteering at the local shelter, still be president of the computer club, still be teasing his little sister, still be in line for hazelnut coffee with whipped cream. He would be alive on the earth, feeling the wind, appreciating the sky, every sense alert to this early spring day. Instead, he was in the ground. He had been her boyfriend and he had died for her. And he'd never known she was going to dump him for Jake.

She'd never even had a date before crushing on Evan. She'd just been plain Amy Cahill, the straight-A student in jeans and sneakers. Unremarkable and overlooked. She wasn't the kind of girl boys noticed. Then she'd looked at Evan, and he'd looked back.

She'd thought she was in love. Until she met intense, charismatic Jake Rosenbloom, and realized that she hadn't had a clue what falling in love was really about.

If only she could remember the exhilaration she'd felt when she'd first realized that Jake loved her back. Now there was so much sorrow and guilt in her heart that she felt as though she was surrounded by fog.

She got up in the morning, brushed her teeth, and did her lesson plans. She and her brother, Dan, now were homeschooled by their former guardian, Nellie Gomez, and several tutors. It had been a rainy fall and a cold winter. The days had dissolved into grays. The books that had once given her comfort had blurred in front of her eyes. Italian lessons, history lessons, math problems, essays, projects.

For the past six months, she'd barely left the house except to run long, hard, cross-country miles. At night she wandered the house, second-guessing every decision she'd made during the battle with the criminal organization the Vespers. When had she gone wrong? Should she have refused to let Evan help them? Should she have ordered Mr. McIntyre back to the US? So many people she had loved had died. She had the clout to force them out of harm's way, but she hadn't.

Why hadn't she used that power?

At sixteen years old, Amy was head of the Cahills, the most powerful family in the world. Their ancestor, Gideon Cahill, had formulated an extraordinary serum at the beginning of the sixteenth century. Since that time, the five branches of the family had battled, spied, lied, stolen, betrayed — all for one purpose only.

Each of the branches had one part of the serum. If the complete serum was assembled, it would make anyone who took it the most powerful person in the world.

After all those hundreds of years, Amy and Dan had been the first to put together the formula for the serum. But they and the other young members of the Cahill family had realized at last that the serum was too incredibly dangerous to even think about producing. Now the formula — a list of thirty-nine ingredients, their complicated calibration, and precise amounts — was safely locked away.

In the steel-trap brain of her thirteen-year-old brother.

Amy's gaze drifted to her sandy-haired brother. Hard to believe that this skinny person now secretly slipping a worm into Aunt Beatrice's purse could be the most powerful kid in the world.

Protecting him — protecting *all* of the Cahills — was her job as head of the family.

Guess I didn't do so well with you, Mac, Amy said to the marble urn, her eyes filling with tears. *Murdered in a hotel room in Rome.*

She wiped her eyes. She had waited six months to bury the ashes of Mr. McIntyre. He was her last tie to security.

Mr. McIntyre had been more than her attorney; he'd been her best and most trusted adviser, and maybe her best friend.

Now here they stood, the only mourners except for Aunt Beatrice, who had started off the morning complaining that her hay fever was acting up and the funeral director had better "get this show on the road."

The elegant marble box sat on a small table. It contained what was left of Mr. McIntyre. Just ashes. His kindness, his shrewdness, his intelligence — it was all gone from the world. Now there was just a box.

The funeral director, whom Dan kept referring to behind his back as "Mr. Death," had shown up late. He nervously wiped at the sweat on his forehead with a handkerchief. When he'd placed the marble box on the table, he'd almost dropped it.

"Is this his first funeral?" Dan whispered.

The tall, muscular clergyman looked more like a football coach. He'd brought a bouquet of wilted red roses. Not Mr. McIntyre's style at all. Amy didn't know whether to laugh or cry. This whole thing just felt surreal. She almost expected Mr. McIntyre to drive up and get out of a long black limousine and say "April Fool."

"This is a disgrace," Aunt Beatrice muttered. "Only three people at the service!"

"Henry Smood is in the hospital with appendicitis," Amy said, referring to Mr. McIntyre's law partner and their new attorney. "He was really upset that he couldn't make it. And the hospital wouldn't release Fiske."

Aunt Beatrice sniffed. "I was talking about *family*,"

she said. "It used to be when a faithful retainer was buried, the Cahills showed up. Even if we despise each other, we used to know how important appearances are."

"Aunt Beatrice buried her *retainer*?" Dan whispered to Amy. "I just flushed mine down the toilet."

Amy stepped on his foot. Her brother made jokes when he was nervous, or scared. She was used to it, but Aunt Beatrice was not.

"Mr. McIntyre *was* family," Amy said.

"Dear," Aunt Beatrice replied, "only *family* is family."

Amy jerked her head away. Aunt Beatrice was tipping the ceremony from difficult to unbearable.

"The Templeton Cahills always used McIntyre and Smood," Aunt Beatrice went on. "And the Durham Cahills. And surely the Starlings could have showed up! Denise Starling used McIntyre for *years* until she decided he was too close to Grace and sent him that poison pen letter. Even if it *was* real poison, she should have let bygones be bygones. And Debra used him for her prenup with that nasty man with the strange name. Never should have married him in the first place . . ."

Aunt Beatrice droned on, naming Cahills Amy and Dan had never heard of. "They didn't come because I didn't invite them, Aunt Beatrice," Amy interrupted.

"But Mr. McIntyre was the family lawyer!" Aunt Beatrice sputtered. She narrowed her beady eyes at Amy. "Did you even *tell* anyone what you were doing?"

"No," Amy said. "I'm not interested in their opinions. I made the decision."

Aunt Beatrice opened her mouth, but Amy held up her hand. "And that's final."

Aunt Beatrice's mouth closed and opened like a fish feeding.

"Way to go," Dan muttered.

Amy gave a small smile. Sometimes it was difficult to be the head of the family, but when it came to Aunt Beatrice, she didn't have a problem.

"Are we ready to begin?" the funeral director whispered. Amy saw him sneak a glance at his watch before gazing down respectfully. She could almost picture him saying, "Dudes, let's get this show on the *road.*"

The clergyman read a Bible verse in a wooden voice. Then he closed the book and nodded at Amy.

"Good-bye, Mr. McIntyre," Amy said. "You were our protector and our friend. The best of the best. Rest in peace."

"Good-bye, Mac," Dan said. "Sorry about the time I put a frog down your pants. Thanks for taking care of us."

Aunt Beatrice sneezed.

The clergyman gestured at the pile of dirt by the open grave. "Would you like to throw a handful of dirt into the grave?" he asked.

"Oh, for heaven's sake. I have *gardeners* for that sort of thing," Aunt Beatrice said. "I have an allergist appointment."

Amy bent down and threw dirt into the grave. Dan did the same. The clergyman handed her the roses and she dropped those in, too. *Sorry, Mac,* she told him silently. *I know you'd prefer tulips.* A sudden memory came to her, of Mr. McIntyre in Grace's garden in his shirtsleeves on a fine May day, regarding a bed of yellow tulips, saying, *Now* there's *a cheerful flower!*

Tears filled her eyes and she almost asked Aunt Beatrice for a tissue, but her aunt had already stalked off. Her driver was hurrying to open the car door.

Mr. Death had left, too — he was almost running as he made his way through the gravestones to his car.

That's odd, Amy thought. *Why did the funeral director leave so quickly? He didn't even say good-bye.*

The clergyman leaned over to pick up the shovel. Amy didn't think she could bear seeing the grave filled up.

As she turned away, something hard hit the back of her head. Pain blinded her, and she felt herself shoved into the open grave.

CHAPTER 2

Amy hit the ground on her hands and knees, feeling the shock shudder through her bones. She looked up. The light was blocked out as a heavy object came flying down at her. She moved by instinct rather than thought, rolling herself into a ball against the wall of the grave.

Dan landed with a cry. She heard his breath leave his body in a soft *uh.* .

"HELP!" Amy shouted.

In answer, a shovelful of dirt rained down on her upturned face. She spat it out.

"Are you okay?" she asked her brother.

He nodded, his face white with pain and fear. His breath was short, and he dug into his pocket for his inhaler. Dan had asthma, and Amy could see the clouds of fine dirt hanging in the air, settling down to choke his airway.

She shouted for help again, but all she saw was the glint of the shovel as more dirt rained down.

"He pushed me in," Dan said, choking and wheezing. "Deliberately . . ."

This can't be happening!

Panic shuddered through her. Her mind whirled. They had no enemies anymore. They had united the family, they had decimated a global criminal organization. They had gone back to being two kids living in a mansion that was too big for them, haunted by all the things they had done and seen. Their only enemies were memories.

So why was this happening again? The horror of it spooled out, making her brain operate on white noise. She couldn't seem to think, or breathe.

Amy was hit by another barrage of soil. Whoever was trying to bury them was working fast and methodically, not even bothering to peek over the edge.

It doesn't matter who's doing it. You have to get out of here.

Amy could feel the dirt in her hair and down her collar and in her ears. She remembered the pile by the open grave. How long would it take before they were covered? How long would it take to suffocate, until the dirt filled her mouth and her ears and her eyes . . .

It's fifth-grade math all over again, she thought crazily. *If the man can scoop a shovelful every ten seconds, and the grave is six feet deep . . .*

"Amy!" Dan's pale face was suddenly sharp as the buzz of panic cleared. He placed an urgent hand on her sleeve. "We've got to get out of here!"

Her brain kicked in at last. Instinct clicked with experience; everything speeded up and she felt very clear. She looked around, assessing, planning. She measured the grave with a quick glance. Probably three square feet. The sides were steep. Amy tried to climb, but the dirt crumbled in her hands. She tried to jam in a toe, but she couldn't get up. Okay, next plan.

"Watch out!" Dan slammed into her, knocking her sideways as the marble box was tossed into the grave as well. It missed Amy's skull by a fraction of an inch and landed on Dan's foot. He let out a grunt of pain and bent over.

Now it was just the two of them and Mr. McIntyre's ashes.

Amy eyed the box. It wasn't just a box. It was a step. It was about a foot high, just what she needed. It was a chance. She'd only get one.

"Dan," Amy whispered. "Get on the urn. Hurry!"

Dan knew what she wanted him to do without her even asking. He balanced on the box. He bent down slightly, making a cradle of his fingers.

Amy looked up, timing her move. One, two, three and she was up, hands on his shoulders; then, using the side of the grave to keep her steady, she balanced, crouching on his shoulders. She felt Dan's body shaking with her weight. He had to hold on, just hold on for three more seconds. She was counting on the machine-like efficiency of their attacker, the precision of his timing as he used the shovel. *Two, one . . .*

She straightened and jumped just as the glint of the shovel went over the lip of the grave. The metal edge glanced against her head — more pain, thank you very much — but she grabbed at it and yanked hard, then fell backward into the grave as Dan flattened himself against the side.

She crashed to her knees, stunned and bleeding — but she had the shovel.

A face appeared against the rectangle of blue sky. The man had ripped off the clergyman collar. He flashed a smile, his teeth white and even.

"Nice work, missy. You got your little toy. Going to dig yourself even deeper?"

The face disappeared. They heard the sound of retreating footsteps. He would be back.

No time to hesitate, no time to press some cloth against the blood on her forehead, only time to wipe it out of her eyes. She jumped back on the marble box, grabbed the shovel by the long handle, and shoved it into the side of the grave, as hard as she could. The shovel fell out, the loose dirt unable to hold it. It had to go deeper.

"Help me, Dan!" He got behind her, and together, grasping the handle, they forced it tightly into the side of the earth. Dan held the shovel and nodded at her. His green eyes were bright against the dirt and blood mixed on his face.

"I've got you," he told her. "Go."

It had to be her, they both knew that. She was a rock climber, a scrambler, she knew how to find the tiny niches, how to plant her body against the wall and get up. She hoisted herself up on the shovel handle and dug her fingers into the earth, closing her eyes as she made a ledge for her fingertips. Dan yanked out the shovel and she hung there while he jammed it a foot higher. She heard him panting hard and fast. She tested the handle.

"Ready?"

"GO!" Dan grunted, and she used the handle to spring up, up to the top of the hole. Every muscle was straining, but she knew she could do it. *Had* to do it. Her hands smacked down over the edge. Her arm muscles quivered as she quickly scanned the cemetery. The man was now about fifty yards away. He was running toward the utility shed. Behind him another man emerged, holding a shovel.

Amy gathered every particle of strength she had and hauled herself over the edge. Her face hit the dirt. She had time to grab one breath — only one — before she found her feet.

Something made her attacker turn, some flicker at the corner of his eye, and he saw her. Both men spurted into a run. Straight at her.

She made a swift calculation. They were fast, much faster than she expected. There was no way she would have time to get Dan out. She had to lead them away.

She streaked down the hill. She felt the benefit of pushing herself through all those punishing runs. Dan had pointed out that they were safe now, she didn't have to be quite so . . . intense, but Amy had found solace in those dawn runs. Now they would help her.

She led them down a sloping hill, leaping over gravestones. All the while she was searching frantically for help, her gaze sweeping the cemetery for any sign of people. They wouldn't attack her if there were people around. She hoped.

She was almost at the Tolliver plot now. She had miscalculated. They were almost on top of her. How could they be so *fast*? She'd had such a big lead!

Amy leaped over a crumbling old headstone, and she felt rather than heard the displacement of air as the shovel was raised. With a sudden swerve, she doubled back and saw the second man's look of surprise as she headed straight toward him with a classic spinning kick, right at his throat.

She connected *hard*.

Why didn't he go down? He wasn't even *winded*.

He just spun away and lifted the shovel, and she ducked at the last minute. It crashed down on the polished granite behind her. The wooden handle snapped, but the steel end of the tool cracked the edge of the stone.

VAN JOSEPH TOLLIVER

The sight of Evan's desecrated stone gave her such a spurt of rage that she picked up the chunk of splintered rock and threw it at the man's head. Blood spurted from his mouth. He smiled. She had a confused impression of eyes the color of the gravestones, blood streaking perfect white teeth.

He raised the splintered end of the handle. She dropped down behind Evan's stone as the man charged. Evan would protect her, one last time.

The handle hit the stone and cracked, and she was off and running before he could grab it again. He was on her heels. She could hear his breathing. So close. She knew any second he would grab her hair, crash into her, and bring her down. . . . And now she saw the other one ahead of her, knees bent and ready, waiting for whatever direction she would choose to go. They would run her down, and for some reason that she would never know, they would kill her, and then they would go back for Dan.

Suddenly, she saw a car turn into the cemetery road, a bright red Toyota. It was the best sight in the world. People.

Amy veered at the last second and started down the hill, leaping over gravestones, waving her arms, and shrieking, "HEY!"

The car pulled over. A youngish woman got out. Amy was confused when, instead of helping, she began to take pictures of Amy with a long-lensed camera.

Another car pulled in. Now Amy was truly confused. Two men got out and began shooting her as well. What was going on?

Her attackers seemed to simply melt away. One moment they were right on her heels, and the next they were almost at a black car, walking quickly, like mourners eager to go home.

Amy turned and ran back toward McIntyre's grave. She lay flat and looked down at Dan. "They're gone. Are you okay?"

Dan's face was a pale oval. She saw the strain around his mouth and knew how afraid he'd been that someone else would be returning. "Sure. I've been buried alive. Never better."

"Wait. I'll get a ladder." She hurried down the hill to the utility shed. To her relief, there was a ladder leaning against the side. She hoisted it and quickly returned to Dan. Amy slid the ladder into the hole and a second later her brother clambered up.

"Do I look as bad as you do?" Dan asked. "Because you look like a zombie. Which I guess makes sense considering we just climbed out of a grave . . ."

A bright yellow Jeep turned into the cemetery, going too fast. Amy grinned. There was only one person she knew who could be late for a funeral and then speed in a cemetery. Nellie.

CHAPTER 3

Dan felt his legs shaking as they jogged toward Nellie's car. He quickly dove into the backseat of the Jeep as Amy climbed into the front. He didn't want them to know how terrified he'd been, waiting those long minutes at the bottom of a grave.

"Kiddos! I'm so sorry! Did I miss everything?" Nellie twisted around and was rooting through the contents in the back, trying to straighten out her usual jumble, which Dan considered an impossible task. The familiarity of the gesture, the usual smell of the car — What was it, exactly? A mixture of popcorn, apples, and that bottle of wheatgrass shampoo Nellie had spilled a year ago? — whatever it was, it helped him feel safe.

When Nellie had returned to college in the winter session, she'd tried for a few days to tone down her look, but now her hair was back to its usual crazy style, jet-black with bleached platinum ends. She was always late, but she claimed it was because she was "mad overscheduled." In addition to tutoring them, she took a full load of classes at Boston University, juggled at least two boyfriends, and cooked at a café in Boston on Wednesday and Saturday nights. Dan grinned when he saw her struggle to sweep her chaos off the backseat onto the floor: On her arm was a new temporary tattoo. The word *FOCUS* blared at him from her tanned forearm.

Nellie had once been their au pair, which meant he had once had the greatest au pair in the history of civilization. She'd traveled the world with them on the hunt for the 39 Clues, watching out for them and protecting them. Now she was like a mashup of older sister and best friend.

Nellie swept the various items—a water bottle, a towel, a cookbook, a bag of apples—off the seat while she talked.

"I had one freaky morning," she said, tossing a half-eaten sandwich back in a paper bag. "My phone got wonky—it ate all my photos!—and then your Uncle Fiske called—he's doing okay, but I think we should go visit—and then I completely *forgot* that I had put cinnamon rolls in the oven, and I *raced* to get here on time, even though I knew Auntie Beatrice would give me the hairy eyeball if I was late . . . and then this red car sideswiped me. . . ." Nellie's head popped up. "Hey, I think that's the car!" she cried, pointing to the red Toyota. Then, finally, she caught sight of Amy and Dan. "Why are you both so dirty? Is that BLOOD?"

"We're okay," Amy reassured her, reaching back for the towel.

"You are most definitely NOT! What happened?"

"I'll tell you while we drive," Amy said. "There's a whole bunch of photographers here, for some reason. Maybe somebody famous is getting buried today." Amy wiped her face and then tossed the towel to Dan.

Nellie put the car into gear and headed toward the cemetery gates. "Okay, spill, because I am about to totally freak out on you. Did you fall out of a tree or something?"

"We fell into a grave," Dan said. "Because we were pushed. Then some goon tried to bury us alive."

"Two of them chased me across the cemetery," Amy added.

Nellie almost swerved off the road as she turned to look at Dan. "That's not funny."

"I didn't think it was, either," Dan said, wiping the last of the dirt off his face.

Nellie's hands gripped the steering wheel. He saw her face change. She, like them, was a Madrigal, the branch of the family that was now in charge of all the Cahills.

"Any idea who they were?" she asked.

"We don't know," Amy said. "That's the trouble." She gazed out the window. "It's starting again, Nellie. I can feel it."

Nellie gave her a quick glance. "What?"

"Some darkness we can't see. It's coming for us. Again."

"Are you *positive* it wasn't just some random crazy guys . . ."

Dan could see Amy's face in the rearview mirror. He knew that look. She was going back over the details, thinking about every word, every gesture. She shook her head firmly. "No. This was targeted. They must have paid off the funeral director. And . . ."

"They knew who we were," Dan said. "I'm sure of it."

"Cahills gone rogue?" Nellie asked.

Amy and Dan considered this. Even though now the family of Cahills had agreed on peace, and their digital network had linked all the branches, they didn't know every Cahill personally.

"I don't think so," Amy said slowly. "There was something . . . professional about these guys. Like hired muscle."

"*Muscle* is the word," Dan agreed. "That was no minister. I thought it was weird that he looked like a buff version of the Incredible Hulk."

"Whoever they were, these guys were Olympic-caliber athletes," Amy said. "When I kicked the guy, it was like slamming into a wall."

Nellie chewed on her lip. "We'll figure it out," she said.

Her voice was confident, but Dan knew that when Nellie chewed on her lip, she was seriously freaked. They were quiet for the rest of the drive.

They drove through the back roads of Attleboro

until they came to the Cahill property. Nellie punched in the code for the iron gates and they pulled into the winding drive. As soon as the gates closed behind them, Dan relaxed. He realized that his hands had been curled into fists.

Grace's elegant mansion loomed ahead, across a meadow and behind a stand of trees. Dan let out a long breath. Home.

Nellie pulled up by the kitchen door and turned off the engine. "Let's hit the Cahill network and see if there are any alerts."

Hanging up their jackets in the mudroom, they took the back stairs two at a time. They didn't use much of the house now — mostly the kitchen, the bedrooms, and Grace's library, a place where they often congregated in the late afternoons, with a fire in the fireplace, Amy's head drooping over a book. Dan had heard her walking the house at night. He knew there was nothing he could do to break her sadness.

I'm one of the richest kids on the planet, and I'm helpless.

Two years ago, after the hunt for the 39 Clues, Amy had unfurled a grand plan to refurbish their grandmother's mansion. She knew trouble was coming and so she built a command center, with a whole bunch of guest rooms and bathrooms and a separate kitchen, in case Cahills had to bunk in and stay over.

Amy had even bought an orbiting satellite for all their communication needs, which she named *Gideon* after the first Cahill. It helped to have a gazillion dollars. Amy wasn't the type of girl to buy sweaters and purses. She bought *satellites*. That just about made her the coolest sister in the galaxy, he figured.

Now Dan used the command center computer to keep at least two chess games going at the same time with his best pal, Atticus Rosenbloom, who lived in Rome with his brother, Jake. Dan knew that something wasn't quite right with his sister and Jake now, but he would rather eat a dish of salamander jelly than ask her about it.

As he walked into the room he saw immediately that he'd been checkmated. Atticus had left a message: *LOSER*.

Beaten by an eleven-year-old. Well, at least Atticus was a genius. He'd graduated from high school and had already been accepted at Harvard, Yale, and the University of Chicago. Dan typed back: *NOT FOR LONG*.

He saw his sister flinch as she crossed the threshold. He knew this room reminded her of Evan.

Saladin rubbed against his ankles and he picked him up. He settled the cat in his lap as he sat at the main computer. He began checking the Cahill feed.

"Nothing out of the ordinary," he reported. He let out a small sigh of relief. At least their family was intact.

Nellie sat at a second computer, a frown on her face. "Your personal alert system is going crazy, though. Look at all these hits."

Amy leaned over her shoulder. "It's a gossip site," she said, surprise in her voice.

Nellie clicked on the link, and an image sprang to life. Amy and Dan in front of Interpol headquarters.

CAHILL BRATS STEAL ART FOR KICKS! screamed the headline. Underneath, in smaller type, it said: *Claim That Thefts Were "Just Pranks." Did They Bribe Their Way to Freedom?*

"*What?*" Amy exclaimed.

"We never said the thefts were pranks!" Dan protested. "And we didn't bribe anybody! Interpol totally got that we only stole stuff to rescue hostages!"

"And they agreed to keep the story quiet," Amy said. "So how did a gossip site get this photo?"

Nellie swallowed. "I took that picture. My phone was hacked!"

"But that was only this morning!" Amy pointed out.

"I *noticed* it this morning," Nellie corrected, her voice grim as she clicked through more links. "It could have happened weeks or even months ago. I hardly ever use that camera."

CAHILL KIDS SKATE AWAY ON THEFT CHARGES

The photograph was taken a few years ago, of Dan and Amy Rollerblading.

"That's my photo for sure," Nellie said. She began to type frantically. "I've got to get our genius tech guy on this."

Dan nudged Nellie over so that he could take her place at the keyboard of the computer. "Look at this," he said. "It's from today."

Amy saw a photograph of herself leaping over a tombstone. Her mouth was open, her hair was flying, and it looked as though she was laughing. She knew the moment that photograph had been taken. She'd been shouting at the young woman who'd raised the camera to her face. But matched with the headline, it looked as though she was having the time of her life.

AMY SEZ: "GHOULS ARE COOL!"

CAHILL KIDS CHOOSE HISTORIC CEMETERY FOR WILD PARTY

"We're like the poster children for the rich and bratty," Amy said. "How did this *happen*?"

Dan clicked through to the next photo, then quickly clicked past it. "This is all just compost. No need to look at it."

"What was that? Come on, I've already seen the worst." Amy hit the BACK button.

She gave a sharp intake of breath when Evan's face appeared.

THE TRAGIC DEATH THAT HAUNTS AMY

Did she cause her first love's death?

Dan looked at his sister's stricken face. Quickly, he clicked away again.

"It doesn't matter what it says. It's just trash."

"They're just trying to drive traffic," Nellie said. "Not enough going on with celebrities in Hollywood, so they found a new target. What I'm wondering is why you two. And why the attack today."

"Do you think they're connected?" Amy asked.

"They're both attacks, aren't they?" Nellie said, taking the keyboard away from Dan. She began clicking and dragging. "One is on you physically, the other on your reputations."

Nellie quickly compiled the stories into a spreadsheet. Dan watched her drag and drop, looking for a pattern.

"Let's plug these sites and tabloids into a search engine and see who the parent companies are," Nellie said.

Within minutes, the results came back.

"They're all owned by one media conglomerate," Amy said. "Founders Media."

"Never heard of it," Dan said.

"It's owned by some rich guy named J. Rutherford

Pierce," Nellie said. "I didn't know he owned his own media company."

"You've heard of him?" Amy asked.

"Sure," Nellie said. "I mean, not my thing—if you're not on the Cooking Channel, I don't know who you are, basically—but he's some kind of major political pundit. He has his own TV and radio shows, and his Twitter feed has over a million followers. Haven't you heard of 'Piercers'?"

At Amy's and Dan's blank looks, she turned back to the computer keys again.

"It's what he calls his followers. 'Piercers.' His show is called *Piercing Intellect*. They have this rah-rah Founding Fathers cult. Look, don't get me wrong, the Founders were seriously cool dudes, but if you think about it, what would they know about, you know, climate change or European debt or . . ."

"Nellie?" Dan spun a fast circle in his chair. "Losing us."

"Here—Pierce's bio."

Amy scanned it quickly. "Born in Maine, was the fourth generation to get into Harvard . . . but look, his business résumé isn't so great if you read between the lines. Three companies he worked for went bust. And then he ran for state senator and lost. . . ."

"Two kids, Galt and Cara—hey, they're our ages, thirteen and sixteen—and a wife, Debi Ann," Dan said. He studied her picture. "Helmet hair."

"He bought a newspaper and that's how he built his fortune," Nellie continued. "Look, this is standard PR stuff. It doesn't give us the real deal. We'll have to dig for that."

"Look at the dates," Dan said. "He bought that one newspaper ten years ago. But suddenly within the last six months he's been acquiring things like magazines and TV stations and websites. . . ."

"You're right, Dan," Nellie said. "He built a media empire in less than a year. How do you do that? He must be a mega-genius."

"A mega-genius who couldn't make it through Harvard," Dan said. "He finished up at Springfield Polytechnic Community College. Where his dad built the new state-of-the-art aqua center."

"There's plenty of information," Nellie said. "But it doesn't say much at all. And it sure doesn't answer why he's targeting you."

Dan spun around in his chair three times. Then he stopped himself with one hand on the desk.

"We're not going to find out just sitting here," he said. "We should just ask the dude."

"You don't just get to a guy like that," Amy said. "You have to go through about seven assistants and a bunch of receptionists, and then he says no."

"So, we ambush him," Dan said.

Amy nodded. "We'd have to track his routine . . . pick a likely coordinate. . . . It's doable, but it will take some surveillance."

"I love it when you talk like a spy kid," Dan said. "Or, we could just show up HERE." He reached over Nellie's shoulder to enlarge one of the windows on the computer.

RUTHERFORD PIERCE TO LEAD REPORTERS ON TOUR OF FOUNDERS MEDIA HEADQUARTERS SITE IN DOWNTOWN BOSTON.

Protests planned.

"Can we make it to Boston in time?" Amy asked.

Nellie grinned. "If I'm driving, we can."

CHAPTER 4

They jumped into the Jeep and Nellie gunned the car down the long, curving drive. She punched in the code and the electric gates swung open.

Cars were now parked on the grassy edges of the lane, slanted in crazy angles. Photographers sprang forward, their faces obscured by cameras.

The noise of camera shutters clicking sounded like hundreds of crickets on a still summer night. "Duck!" Nellie yelled.

Amy ducked, but not before seeing a camera snapping a picture of her frightened face.

Nellie gunned the motor and sped past them. Still clicking, the photographers ran for their cars.

"Can you lose them?" Amy asked. Her heart pounded. She felt hunted and trapped.

"Are you kidding?" Nellie sped down the street, then made a short right turn onto a dirt road. She squeaked past overgrown shrubbery to barrel down a driveway. "The Fieldstones won't mind," she said. "I gave Marylou my coffee cake recipe." She swerved off the driveway, bumped over a grassy field, skirted a badminton net, then made a hard right onto a back road that ran along a lake. "We can get to the highway from here."

Nellie made several fast turns and approached the highway. She swung the car into the turning lane under the BOSTON sign.

"You see?" she said confidently. "All clear."

Dan twisted behind her. "Um, not. I think I see that red Toyota again. And a couple others. They must have made a guess that we might be headed to the city."

The drive was short and tense. Nellie went as fast as she dared, but cars kept swerving close, trying to get a picture. The photographers cut across three lanes of traffic, hung out of windows shooting, popped out of sunroofs.

"There's some hats back there," Nellie said. "Try to cover your faces so they can't take your picture. Maybe they'll give up."

Dan pawed through the hats. He held up a Mexican sombrero. "Uh, Nellie?"

"Free Hat Night at Don Jose's Cantina," Nellie explained. "You gotta try the chimichangas."

"Haven't you ever heard of Cap Day at the stadium?" Dan grumbled. He pulled on a plaid winter hat with earflaps and handed Amy a canvas beach hat. She pulled it down to her eyebrows. She couldn't hear the clicking of the shutters but she felt their intrusive chatter hammering inside her brain.

Nellie jerked the wheel suddenly to the right and exited off the highway, leaving two cars full of photographers zooming past, comical looks of surprise on their faces.

"See ya, suckers!" Nellie called as she gunned through a yellow light, made two successive quick left turns, and then plunged into the notorious Boston traffic.

After a few minutes of combat driving, Nellie pulled up in a bus lane with a cry of satisfaction. "I rule Beantown!"

They craned their necks and looked straight up at the skeleton of a skyscraper across the street.

FOUNDERS MEDIA

COMMUNICATION • SYNERGY • CONNECTION

YOUR FUTURE IS OUR PRESENT

A bus driver leaned on the horn behind them. "Text me when you're done," Nellie said. "I'll meet you right here."

Ignoring the blaring horn, Nellie scanned the sidewalk. "There's a lot of security. How are you going to sneak in?"

"Just follow my first rule of life," Dan said as he slid out of the Jeep. "Everybody's gotta eat."

Fifteen minutes later, Amy and Dan walked to the side construction entrance, both carrying bags from Brown Bag Subs. The tantalizing aroma of meatball subs snaked up from the bags.

Three construction workers sat on a makeshift bench of two-by-fours and bricks, right outside a door marked CONSTRUCTION SITE: DO NOT ENTER.

"You guys know Joe?" Dan asked, holding up the bag. "This is his order."

"Just go through the door and yell," one of the guys said. "He should be in the office."

Amy and Dan pushed through the door. "How did you know a guy named Joe worked here?" Amy asked as they dropped the food bags on a table.

"That's my second rule of life," Dan said. "There's always a guy named Joe." He grabbed a yellow hard hat and tossed one to Amy.

"It's starting to scare me how much you know about breaking and entering," Amy observed, putting it on.

They stood in the hall, wondering which way to go. The building had girders and beams and drywall that marked a few rooms. Stacks of wood and glass littered the space, along with rolls of insulation and long snakelike bundles of rebar. Plastic buckets held empty coffee cups and scraps of metal and wood. Spray-painted in orange on the walls were mysterious letters and numbers. Large concrete columns marched down the space, and the dust spiraled in the air through the beams of light.

"I smell something," Dan said.

"Danger?" Amy asked.

"Does danger smell like cookies?"

Amy sniffed the air. "And coffee."

"If there's a tour, there might be coffee for the press," Dan said. "Maybe we can mingle and we won't get noticed."

Following their noses, they moved toward the front of the building. Soon they could hear murmuring voices.

"These are stale," someone said.

"Hey, they're free. Coffee's not bad."

Amy and Dan peered around the wall. About a dozen reporters stood scarfing down cookies and gulping coffee out of paper mugs.

They sidled in and lingered at the edge of the group.

"Where are you from?" one of the reporters asked Dan. He had spiky red hair and looked almost as young as they did.

"Uh . . . a national kids' magazine," he answered. *"Homeschooling Monthly."*

The guy nodded. "Sounds cool. Wish I'd been homeschooled. Just not with, you know, my own parents. I'm with the web 'zine *Celebrity Dish.*"

"Isn't that owned by Founders Media?" Amy asked. "So, Mr. Pierce is kind of your boss?"

He shrugged. "We're all part of the company. Your

magazine, too—you just don't know it. You think this guy wants bad press? He's already got a stack of violations on this building. He's throwing shade on a community garden—did you see the protestors? And some poor construction guy got killed last month. They're putting this up so fast they've got safety inspectors breathing down their necks . . . but then they mysteriously go away. Hey, do you have your question ready? We're only allowed one each, you know. I'm going to ask what color pajamas he wears."

"You're going to ask about *pajamas*?" Dan blurted.

"I'm not going for a Pulitzer here, buddy. I just want to keep my job. If Pierce says polka dots, I've got a headline."

"Love that hard-hitting news," Dan muttered.

A trim young woman in a red suit entered the space, her high heels clicking. She was wearing, Dan noticed, a small headset tucked under her hair, a slender silver wire hovering near the corner of her mouth.

"Hi, guys! I'm Arabella Kessler. I'm Mr. Pierce's personal assistant, and I'll be escorting you from the hospitality suite to the reception suite." She waved her yellow hard hat. "Let's all put on our hats! Now follow me to the sixty-fifth floor!"

They followed Arabella Kessler and her clicking heels to a large cage elevator on the side of the building. The reporters filed inside. The cage rose up, up, high over the city. A gust of wind shook the wire mesh cage. Some of the reporters turned green. "Best view in Boston," Arabella said, and pushed open the door.

They filed out into a space similar to the ground floor. Concrete, piles of stacked glass, machinery lying idle. Wires hung down from the grid of the ceiling, coiled like snakes about to strike.

A room had been framed out with metal columns. At one end a podium had been set up, with red drapes hung behind it. The wind blew through the open space. Even though they were nowhere near the edge, Amy shivered. The reporters clustered together nervously. Everyone felt exposed, so high above the city, with no walls for protection.

Arabella Kessler stood behind the podium and spoke into the microphone. Her voice echoed and bounced from one concrete pillar to another.

"Welcome to the sixty-fifth floor of the new head-quarters of Founders Media, the number one media conglomerate in the United States!"

There was a silence, and then a few claps began. Apparently applause was called for.

"Yes, isn't it thrilling! The innovative design of Founders Media headquarters will include a one-square-block complex with three separate buildings, all joined by pedestrian bridges! The buildings will offer offices, retail, restaurants, and the Founders tele-vision studios. After a short press conference during which you can ask your preapproved questions, you will get a personal tour of the new Founders Media headquarters by J. Rutherford Pierce himself. Ladies and gentlemen, I give you J. Rutherford PIERCE!" She almost screamed his last name.

A tall man with silver hair and a movie-star smile strode through the curtains. The lights bounced off his burnished skin. He looked glowing and healthy and ready to take on the world. "So happy to be here today, my friends!" he said, taking his place at the podium. "I'll take a few questions before we start the tour."

"What is your secret to success?" someone asked.

"Work hard and love your country."

"What do you like to do on your day off?"

"Play with my dog, Sport, and grill some good meat!"

"As long as he doesn't grill Sport," Dan murmured to Amy. The reporter standing next to them overheard and chuckled.

"How do you account for your spectacular rise?"

"I worked hard and I love my country."

Dan groaned into Amy's ear. "Talk about puffball questions. How are we going to get to talk to him?"

"On the tour," she said.

"Not with all these handlers around," Dan said. "I say we shake things up." He raised his voice. "How much does it cost these days to bribe a safety inspector?"

The reporters instantly went quiet. The red-haired reporter turned and frantically motioned at Dan to shut up.

"I mean, does the cost go *up* or *down*, depending on how close you are to finishing the building?" Dan asked.

"Sorry, I didn't catch that." Pierce peered over the crowd but couldn't see Amy and Dan, who were standing behind the taller reporters. His eyes cut to Arabella Kessler, and her sharp gaze raked the crowd.

"Any other questions?" he asked.

"What about the worker who was killed?" Amy asked. "Is it because you're cutting corners on safety?"

The red-haired journalist gave Amy and Dan a look of admiration. Amy saw him square his shoulders. He raised his hand. "And where did his widow get a million dollars, when he didn't have life insurance? Was she paid off?"

"Care to comment on that?" someone else yelled.

Pierce blinked once. Twice. His smile didn't wobble. He swiveled toward Arabella Kessler.

She moved forward quickly as Pierce disappeared behind the red curtain. "We're out of time!" she called cheerily. "Something has come up, and Mr. Pierce must leave us. I'll conduct the tour."

Amy called out, "Hey, what about the photo op?"

The reporters took up the question and began shouting at Arabella Kessler. Amy and Dan quickly moved forward and stepped behind the curtain, looking for Pierce.

"There he goes," Amy whispered.

Just behind a concrete column, they saw Pierce picking his way around a pile of stacked wood flooring.

Maneuvering around pails and tools and rolls of insulation, they tracked Pierce as he moved through the building. They could see that he was heading toward elevators on the east side of the building.

"Mr. Pierce!" Amy yelled, running toward him. "We have a question!"

He turned, his smile frozen in place. Amy saw something flicker across his face when he saw her: recognition.

He knows who we are.

And then a second, more startling thought as his gray eyes stayed on her face.

He hates me.

"And who would you be?" he asked.

"You know who we are," Amy answered. "Amy and Dan Cahill. The kids you've been tormenting in your media outlets."

"I don't have anything to do with the content in my magazines and websites," Pierce said. "That's what the Third Amendment is all about, a free press."

"First Amendment," Amy replied, and noted two spots of red on his cheeks at her correction. "And freedom of the press means that the government can't censor the press. It doesn't mean that you can't forbid your employees from writing sensational and untrue stories just to sell papers."

"But that's my job, selling papers, little lady," Pierce said. "And magazines, and website content. But if you're upset about something, I suggest you contact our press office. It will make its way to the right person."

"*You're* the right person," Dan said. "You're the boss."

Two security guards appeared, wearing baseball caps and tinted glasses. Amy and Dan hadn't heard them approach, but there they were, as solid and unyielding as the concrete pillars around them.

"Hey, fellas," Pierce said to them. "Gosh, this is why we lead a tour, kids. You can't go wandering off by yourself. Construction sites are hazardous places. Accidents can happen so easily when you're sixty-five stories up in a skyscraper without walls. Especially with the two Cahill daredevils! We wouldn't want you to go splat now, would we?"

Amy looked at him, startled. Could he be *threatening* them? Impossible. He was a businessman. A major media celebrity . . .

"Show them the way out, gentlemen," Pierce told the security guards. "The *right* way out, that is."

Dan doubled over and sneezed repeatedly. While Pierce backed up, an expression of distaste on his face at his explosions, Dan dipped his hand into the plastic bucket next to him and then shoved it in his pocket.

Pierce barked at the security goons, "Why are you still standing here?"

One of the guards roughly shoved Dan forward. "Move."

The guards led them in the opposite direction from the reporters. Amy's mind raced. Something wasn't right. Why weren't they being led back to the group?

They were being corralled toward the far end of the building. They emerged from the drywall corridor, and Amy suddenly had a direct line of sight to Pierce. He stood stabbing the elevator button repeatedly. From this position Amy could also see what Pierce could not—the crowd of reporters hurrying toward him, Arabella scurrying behind them, waving her arms. Pierce couldn't see them . . . but he could hear them. She could tell by the frown of irritation on his face.

It happened in a flash. Amy blinked as Pierce grabbed a nearby hanging rope, swung out over empty air, then dropped onto the partially completed pedestrian bridge a story below. He quickly walked over it, sixty-four stories above the city, then stepped into the skeleton of the building next door and disappeared.

What was that? Did the man just drop ten feet, land on a girder . . . and tightrope across it?

"Move it, sister," one of the guards said, nudging her along.

The guards pushed them past a curtain of thick plastic sheeting. Here the construction wasn't as far along as on the rest of the floor. Girders stretched out into empty air. There was no drywall at all, just a concrete floor. Construction equipment surrounded them. A piece of yellow tape acted as a flimsy barrier between them and open air.

"Oops, no elevator. Guess we made a mistake," one of the guards said. "So you're going to have to take the fast way down."

"Are you kidding?" Dan asked.

"I don't know," the guard said with a terrible smile. "Am I?"

The two guards herded them closer to the edge. Amy and Dan had to back up.

"C'mon, you kids are daredevils, right?" the other one said. "Let's see what you can do. If you walk out on the girders, you can almost make it to the building next door. If you jump far enough." He chortled.

They were close to the edge now. Amy didn't want to look down, but she couldn't help it. She could see tiny people moving below, cars and buses that looked like the metal toys Dan used to leave scattered on the floor when he was five.

"You're scaring me!" Dan suddenly said. He shuddered, both hands in his pockets. "I-I'm afraid . . . of heights! NO! NO!" he screamed.

"Shut up, kid!"

Dan moved in a flash. His hand came out of his pocket and he threw ball bearings on the floor between them.

Amy didn't need to be prompted. She knew what Dan was planning without one word being spoken. She and Dan ran in the opposite direction from the wildly rolling balls. They heard the curses of the guards as they windmilled their arms, trying to keep their balance and run at the same time. Both of them crashed to the floor.

Amy and Dan knew they had only seconds before the guards were after them again. They pushed through the thick plastic sheet and took off.

"This way," Dan said, darting down a hallway.

Amy followed without question. She knew that her brother's photographic memory had stored the layout of the floor in his head. He was probably leading them back to the elevator they'd taken to get up here, in hopes that Arabella had finally corralled the reporters. There would be safety in a crowd.

They heard the rustle of the plastic screen, then the *thump-thump* of running footsteps. The guards would be on them at any moment.

Then Amy heard the *whirr* of the elevator. Dan had already spurted toward the sound.

"There they are! Get them!" They heard the guttural voices behind them, but it would waste time to turn. They only had seconds now.

They burst out of the corridor just in time to see the top half of the reporters in the elevator as it descended past the floor.

"Our only chance," Amy said to Dan. "C'mon."

They both raced toward the descending cage and jumped.

Amy felt the cage rattle as she landed. Dan landed next to her. Arabella Kessler screamed, and one of the reporters shouted, "HEY!"

Amy and Dan dropped to their knees and laced their fingers through the mesh. The chilly wind threatened to blow them off the top of the cage.

Amy looked down through the wire cage. Arabella's angry face stared up at her.

"Going down?" Dan asked.

CHAPTER 5

"That went well," Nellie said, fiercely turning the wheel as she exited the highway at Attleboro. "Just a reminder: One is supposed to ride in the *inside* of an elevator. Are you both insane?"

"We were just trying to get away!" Dan protested. "You should have seen those guys! They were trying to kill us!"

"Or scare us," Amy said.

"Scare us to *death*," Dan said. "We could have been pancaked on the pavement!"

Amy shook her head in frustration. "Why did this guy Pierce target us? It's not just to sell papers."

"He recognized us, Amy," Dan said. "Somehow he *knows* us. Did you see the way he looked at you?"

Amy shivered as she remembered that gaze, ice gray and unrelenting. "He hates me. And I never met him before today!"

"Whoa, duck down!" Nellie suddenly yelled. "The vultures are still circling."

A phalanx of cars still waited outside the Cahill

gates. Nellie gunned the motor as the gates swung open and zoomed inside. As soon as they were out of sight, Amy and Dan popped up again.

Dan held out his phone to Amy with a groan. There was a picture on the Exploiter website of Dan and Amy balancing on top of the elevator cage. They were grimacing from the effort of holding on, but it looked like they were smiling. The headline was CAHILL CUTUPS ENDANGER BOSTON PEDESTRIANS FOR KICKS.

Amy dropped her head in her hands. "This is a nightmare. And we don't even have one clue. This guy popped up out of nowhere."

"Everybody has a history," Dan said. He dug into his pocket. "And one of the security guards dropped this." He held up a scrap of paper.

"It's a ticket from the New Jersey Turnpike," Amy said, examining it. "That doesn't tell us much."

"Well, we can place them on the road at a certain date and time," Dan said. "Maybe Pierce was someplace south of New Jersey on that date, and we can go there and do some snooping."

"Worth a try," Amy said.

Nellie's phone pinged as she unlocked the back door. "I hope that's Pony," she said.

"Did she say something about a pony?" Dan asked Amy as they shrugged out of their jackets.

"Our tech guy," Nellie murmured as she read a text. "He's getting back to me on my phone hacking. Pony is *fast*."

"Did she say she has a *fast* pony?" Dan asked. "Why are we the last to know?"

As Nellie punched in a number, Dan and Amy headed up the back stairs to the communications center. When they turned the computers on, a red alert flashed. At the same time they heard the sound of running feet and Nellie burst into the room.

"Shut down the system!" she shouted. "Go to Level Five!"

Quickly Dan ran through the keystrokes. The system was designed to shut down and reboot, as though there had been a power surge. But all the information on the hard drives would be wiped and replaced—names of Cahill contacts, addresses, safe houses—it would all be false, with enough nuggets of truth to fool even the wiliest hacker. Whoever breached the network wouldn't know that the Cahills were onto them.

Nellie leaned over Dan's shoulder as the screen went black, then immediately rebooted.

"I don't know what's going on, but Pony said to shut it down."

Just then Amy's phone buzzed, and she checked the number. She looked inquisitively at Dan. "It's Mr. Smood," she said, naming McIntyre's law partner.

"It's okay, you can talk on your phone, you just can't use e-mail," Nellie said.

"Amy, is that you?" The usual calm tones of Henry Smood were rattled. "I have some unsettling news for you. It appears that you are under federal investigation for embezzlement. They have a search warrant. You have to let them in, but don't answer any questions until I get there. Not one, do you hear me?"

"We haven't done anything wrong! We have nothing to hide."

Mr. Smood cleared his throat. "Ah. And innocent people never go to jail."

"Okay, I get your point," Amy said. "We'll keep our mouths shut."

"All right, hold down the fort. I'm on my way."

"But you just had surgery—"

"Checked myself out. I don't need my appendix. But you need a lawyer."

Amy heard the sharp click of the receiver. She'd never heard Mr. Smood sound so unnerved.

From up here, the knocking wasn't very loud, but it was insistent.

Dan ran to the window. "They're here," he said.

CHAPTER 6

The agents were polite but efficient. They swarmed over the house, paying particular attention to the command center. It was clear that they were both impressed with and suspicious of the complexity of the computer system. They unplugged and carried everything out.

Mr. Smood showed up and sat with Dan and Amy at the kitchen table while the agents carried files and computers out of the house. Nellie made tea and brought out the cinnamon rolls she'd made that morning. No one could eat.

A cold, hard rain began to fall. Finally, the agents left. Meanwhile, the presence of the black federal vehicles had inflamed the paparazzi. They had dared to climb over the stone wall and were set up on the lawn, busily filming and snapping photographs.

"We're prisoners," Amy said, watching behind a curtain as the photographers snapped photos of the agents carrying out boxes and equipment.

The federal agents got into their cars and drove away. Mr. Smood left, promising to get to the bottom of it. Soon even the die-hard paparazzi gave up and hurried to their cars. One by one, the cars drove away.

Amy picked at a roll, smashing the crumbs with her finger. She couldn't remember a time when she'd felt so helpless. Without their computers, they couldn't follow their slender lead.

Someone beat a rhythmic three knocks on the back door. They barely heard it over the rain. Cautiously, Nellie opened it.

A boy of about nineteen stumbled in, his ankle-length raincoat dripping rivers onto the kitchen floor. His hair was pulled back in a stringy ponytail, and his black-framed glasses were steamed. He looked like a cross between a drowned badger and the Loch Ness monster. He held out his arms like Frankenstein, blinded by his foggy glasses.

"Uh, Nellie?"

Nellie reached over and took off his glasses. She polished them on her shirt. "You must be Pony."

"How'd you know?"

"I'm a genius," she said, handing them back to him. "Come on, sit. I'll get you a towel. This is Amy and Dan. Guys, this is Pony — our tech adviser."

"I prefer digital cowboy," Pony said.

"You two have never met?" Amy asked.

"Just online," Pony said, shrugging. "I'm not an analog person."

"Have a seat, pardner," Nellie told him, tossing him several dish towels. As he wiped himself down, she turned back to Amy and Dan. "He set up our system and has been maintaining it ever since. And apparently, we have a problem."

"Mondo problemo," Pony said. His long, mournful face gave him the look of a hound dog, and when he licked his lips while looking at the cinnamon rolls, the resemblance was complete.

Amy pushed the plate toward him. "Help yourself."

He grabbed a roll and finished it in two bites. "Okay. Your lossage is off the charts, but there is hope. I can build the system back—it's just going to take time. Therefore I have brought to you"—he opened his raincoat, revealing a large inner pocket—"this baby," he said, sliding out a small netbook. "It's whistle-clean. And"—he reached inside the deep inner pocket again—"I programmed new smartphones. These are already encrypted, so you can send messages, but even I can't guarantee complete safety, so don't pass anything really crucial until I get a handle on who's targeting you." He popped another roll in his mouth. "Whoever the hacker dude is, he's a stealth machine. Mega wattage. Along with these rolls, by the way."

"What can you tell about him?" Nellie asked.

"He was able to invade a system designed by me. That narrows it down to maybe ten people on the planet."

"Modest much?" Dan asked.

"Dude, there's no modesty in hackery. Are you going to eat your roll?"

Dan pushed over the plate.

Pony stood with the roll halfway out of his mouth. "Now. Let me see the system."

"You can't. Federal agents just took it out an hour ago."

"Oh, man. Seriously?" Pony crashed back into his chair. "This is so bletcherous!" He shuddered. "Okay, reboot . . . hand over your old phones. I might — *might*, I'm saying — be able to track the break-in through them. In my line of work, if you think something is impossible, it is. Until you decide it's possible and you do it."

Amy, Dan, and Nellie pushed over their phones. He dumped them in his inside pocket. Then he dumped the rest of the rolls into his outside pocket and stood. "Adios, amigos," he said. He tromped to the door, opened it, and disappeared into the black rain.

Dan stared after Pony. "Our fate is in the hands of that guy?"

"He's off-the-charts smart," Nellie said, but even she sounded uncertain.

Amy sat, thinking hard. "If you *think* something is impossible, it is," she said. "Until you decide it's possible. Then it's possible. Isn't that what he just said?"

"Sounded like it," Dan said. "If you add half a cinnamon roll to it."

The sense of unease that had been gnawing at her suddenly grew into sheer horror. Information flashed.

Connections clicked. One *impossible* connection after another.

"Amy?" Nellie touched her arm. "Are you okay? You look like you're going to faint." She stood up and put her hand on Amy's neck. "Put your head between your knees. Breathe, kiddo."

"No." Amy's voice was muffled because her head was now between her knees. The terrible truth was staring her in the face. Something she didn't even want to glimpse, let alone confront.

She shook off Nellie's hand and stood. "It can't be!" she said. "It just can't be, but . . ." Her voice trailed off. ". . . I think he did it. Somehow . . ."

"What?" Dan asked. "You're freaking us out, dude."

Amy took a deep breath and faced them.

"Pierce has taken the serum!"

CHAPTER 7

What happens when your worst nightmare has just come true?

Amy couldn't think for a minute. Couldn't breathe. The thought that the serum could be *out there* was too terrifying.

A serum that could make one person all-powerful. J. Rutherford Pierce. Someone with no scruples at all . . .

. . . could become the most powerful person in the world.

Amy's eyes went wide with horror.

He's already well on his way.

That's why he targeted us.

Because we're the only ones who can expose him.

Can stop him . . .

"Amy?" Nellie gripped the table edge. "You're scaring us. Pierce couldn't have taken the serum. It's imposs—"

"No!" Amy smacked her hand down on the table. It was such an unexpected gesture that Dan and Nellie both jumped. "Just listen. There are four branches of the Cahills besides Madrigals. Four separate sets of abilities. Dan, remember how Pierce swung off the building and hit that pedestrian bridge? How does a middle-aged guy *do* that? What did it remind you of?"

"A Tomas," Dan said. The branch, they knew, that had accelerated physical powers. He shook his head. "But—"

Amy shook her head impatiently, unwilling to listen. She had to make them *see.* "And, Nellie—remember what we said—that his rise to fame just defied any sense of *logic*? He fails at one thing after another, and then in less than a year he rises to the top. He leveraged all these buyouts and gobbled up all these companies so fast . . . and got in with politicians and power brokers. . . ."

"Like a strategist. A Lucian," Nellie said. "Okay, but—"

"And how *every* article mentions his out-of-the-box thinking, and how charming he is—he manages to charm millions of people without ever letting someone trip him up! Like a Janus! And now Pony tells us that our absolutely impenetrable fortress of a computer system is breached."

"Ekat," Dan said. "But we've seen what the serum does. When Isabel Kabra took it, she didn't look like a normal human. She was sort of . . . glowing."

"But, Dan, think about it. Pierce wasn't glowing, but he looked . . . I don't know . . . *enhanced.* Did you notice how his skin was sort of golden?"

"Fake tan," Nellie said.

"No." Amy shook her head firmly. "I remember noticing how the lights just bounced off him when he took the podium. *But there were no lights on.* And if it *is* true, the rest makes sense — why he targeted us in the first place. Why he's making us look like . . . like idiotic socialites. Because who would listen to us if we tried to expose him? But now maybe he's going even further — he wants to scare us. Or kill us." Amy turned to Dan. "When those guards told us to walk out on those girders . . . I think they were serious. Don't you?"

Dan gulped and nodded. "I do."

"Amy, I see why you're suspicious, but you're forgetting a detail," Nellie said. "There is no serum. Anywhere in the world. We've made absolutely sure of that. And the only one who knows the formula is Dan."

"I know."

Dan backed away a step. She saw panic in his eyes.

"I didn't tell anyone!"

"I know that," Amy said. "But you *did* assemble it." Six months ago. When he'd thought it was the only way to save the world.

Amy took a deep breath. She didn't want it to be true. She didn't want to trace the serum back to Dan. If he was responsible for the serum getting out, the guilt could crush him. She could see the telltale spots of red on his cheeks that meant he was getting upset.

"I know it's not your fault, Dan," Amy added quickly. "I *know* that. But if the impossible happened — if the serum formula got out somehow — we have to figure out *how*. There could be some random Cahill out there who found it. . . ."

"Unlikely," Nellie said.

Suddenly, Dan collapsed on the floor, his head in his hands. "No," he said, his voice muffled. "It must be me. Somehow."

He looked up at them, tears in his eyes. "Do the math. I fabricated the serum secretly about six months ago. That's right when Pierce began his climb to power."

"Coincidence," Nellie said, but her voice sounded shaky.

Amy got down on the floor next to Dan. She put her hand on her brother's arm. "Tell me what happened in that lab," she said. She'd never asked him for details. She knew he had deeply regretted what he'd done.

Dan's voice shook. "I found all the ingredients myself. And I had heard about our cousin Sammy Mourad — some sort of genius biochemist postdoctoral student at Columbia University. I-I contacted him and asked him to mix up something for me."

He wiped at his cheeks. "But I took all these pre-cautions! I'm not stupid. I gave Sammy *some* of the ingredients, but not all. Only the stuff that had to be done in a lab. Then I took my own vial and mixed the final version myself."

"Where?" Amy asked.

"In Sammy's lab. But I took the dose with me! There was a tiny bit left over, and I threw it down the sink.

There is *no way* anybody could have figured out the formula! Not even Sammy."

Amy shook her head. "There's no other way. Sammy has to be the key. You did everything right, Dan, but somehow . . ."

"But even if somehow, some way, Sammy found out the formula, which I don't believe — why would he pass the formula on?" Dan asked. "He's a Cahill."

"Yeah, and we've seen what towers of integrity Cahills can be," Amy said, with a lift of an eyebrow.

Nellie slid off her chair and landed on the floor next to them. "If it's really out there . . ." she whispered. She couldn't finish the sentence.

The three of them looked at each other. The horror they felt was reflected in each other's eyes.

Nellie swallowed. "We have to send out a Cahill alert. We need help on this."

"Not yet," Amy insisted. "We don't know what we're dealing with yet. First we have to talk to Sammy. In person." She glanced at the clock. "If we leave now, we can be there by eleven P.M."

Nellie stood. "We're on Level Five alert, remember? If we leave the house, it's Endgame. Grab your gear."

They had established the Endgame strategy soon after returning home from the Vesper battle. If ever they felt in real danger, they had to be prepared to go into hiding. Their backpacks were already packed with the essentials, and they had money belts and passport slings to wear under their shirts.

"Chances are we'll be back. But better safe than sorry," Nellie said. She went into the pantry, where the gear was stowed. She brought the packs and belts back and handed them over.

Silently, they suited up. The word *Endgame* echoed in Amy's head. This was the worst. Everything they feared. Pierce was willing to kill them to get what he wanted.

And what is that? Amy wondered. *If he had all the power in the world, what would he do?*

CHAPTER 8

Somewhere in the Australian outback

The prefab housing was designed to be taken down within minutes. Inside the flexible skin stretched over aluminum rods were rudimentary sleeping quarters but state-of-the-art technology. Satellite-equipped phones, computers, tablets. Emergency generators. And a box of thermonuclear devices.

The dust swirled around three men as they walked from a military helicopter to the first building. The heat was a blunt force, bouncing off the flat, scorched land and slamming against exposed skin.

The short, muscled man with a red beard was flanked by the two taller men. One of them wore sunglasses and a shoulder holster with an automatic weapon. The other was tall, lanky, and kept nervously pushing up his glasses with a sweaty finger.

The silver-haired man with the Hollywood good looks was already on the screen.

"You're late," he spoke as the three men came into camera view.

"We just exploded a thermonuclear device, Mr. Pierce," the man with the red beard said. "I think we're allowed a little leeway."

"I don't give leeway, Mr. Atlas. Especially when it comes to thermonuclear devices. Results?"

The nervous-looking man pushed up his glasses. "I've sent all the data. Seismic activity log, radiation levels, impact calculations, spec models . . ."

"Any local reactions?"

"Several reports of a flash in the sky, earthquake . . . It made the paper in Perth—"

"We took care of it," Atlas interrupted. "As far as the public knows, it was a meteorite impact."

"Government investigation?"

"We'll take care of that, too. That's what you pay us for." Atlas smiled without humor.

Back in his office in Boston, Pierce concealed his exhilaration. The plan was working! He'd found the group and investigated them thoroughly. Atlas was a former mercenary. He'd developed a global business of testing and selling nuclear weapons. He'd bought various testing sites around the world—roughly a half-million acres in the outback, a couple of uninhabited Pacific islands, and probably some sites Pierce didn't know about—and provided one-stop service for rogue governments, terrorists, and visionaries like Pierce.

"So you keep the weapons until I send word," Pierce continued. "And you can get them where I need them?"

"Anywhere in the globe."

"The evidence . . ."

"Will be planted. Relax, Mr. Pierce. We're here to serve."

"I'll be in touch."

Pierce cut the connection and walked to the window.

He was almost there. The last piece was in place. Years of planning came down to this, and now things would move fast.

The thing was, it was remarkably easy to start a world war. History had taught him that. It just took strategy and enough nerve to order several simultaneous nuclear explosions in key cities around the globe. Plant some evidence, and the next thing you know, governments started accusing. Started mobilizing.

As president, he could escalate the war. And when invasion seemed to threaten and the grateful people looked to him to save them, he would take complete control. The world would beg him to take absolute power, they would be so grateful.

And then, he would take over the broken world and rebuild it. Soon, only those with absolute loyalty would be able to enjoy the good things in life. Housing, transportation, information. Piercers would be the powerful, and all the world's riches would go to them. The worthy ones.

Only one problem remained. No one could know

about the serum. No one could find out the source of his power.

Once, the fact that the two Cahills managed to outsmart his guards would have ruffled him. No more.

Using his media empire to set them up had been a brilliant stroke. Now the public thought they were silly socialites. Irresponsible daredevils. Accidental deaths wouldn't even be investigated. A few headlines, and it would be over.

He thought back to seeing the girl up close. Her hair was the reddish brown of an autumn leaf . . . so close to the shade her mother's had been. She had the same curve to her upper lip.

When he saw her in person, it was like seeing a ghost. A ghost in a nightmare of shame. Just remembering Hope Cahill made his blood rise. The girl not only looked like her, she was a know-it-all like Hope had been. Seeing her had made him want to smash something, kill something. . . .

Yes, the girl looked so much like her mother.

He smiled. Soon they'd be resting side by side.

CHAPTER 9

New York City

Darkness fell as they drove toward New York City. The windshield wipers marked their progress with a steady *whish, whish.* Dan sat in the back, looking out at a blurred landscape. With every mile, the guilt stabbed him more acutely.

If the serum was loose on the world . . . it was his fault.

If Sammy Mourad had sold the formula . . . it was his fault.

My fault, my fault, my fault.

Whish, whish, whish.

He was staring down a tunnel of horror.

If Pierce really had the serum . . .

. . . the most destructive item known to humanity . . .

. . . *My fault, my fault, my fault.*

Whish, whish, whish.

I can't do this anymore, Dan thought.

Dan had texted Sammy from the car to ask if he was working late and if Dan could bring him a pizza. The returning text was only one word:

PEPPERONI.

Sammy was waiting outside the chemistry building on the Columbia University campus. He stood leaning against a stone wall, not caring about the drizzle. His longish, thick black hair was stirred by the breeze, and his gray sweater was pushed up his forearms. He had a straight nose, a curving half smile, and thick dark brows over liquid black eyes.

"Oh. My. Goodness," Nellie said in three short bursts under her breath. "Dan, you said he was a genius Ekat. You did *not* say he was a work of *art*."

"What?" Dan turned around. Even Amy was staring. "Oh, yeah. Sorry. I didn't think the handsome part was relevant."

"It's always relevant, kiddo," Nellie said.

Sammy came forward, smiling. "Dan! You are the man! Bringing a snack to a starving grad student counts for hero status around here."

Dan handed Sammy the pie. He quickly introduced Nellie and Amy.

Sammy swiped them into the building with his

ID card, and they followed him upstairs to his lab. It was neat and orderly, with stacks of file folders and notebooks. A pyramid of orange soda cans had been connected with purple duct tape and sat on a wide windowsill. Sammy pushed some wheeled stools toward them and swept aside the folders to plop the pizza on the lab table. Then he reached inside a file drawer and came out with paper plates, napkins, oregano, crushed red pepper, and garlic salt.

"The works," he said with satisfaction. "You see the garlic salt? I don't cook with it—I'd rather control the garlic and salt separately. But for pizza, you gotta go with it. It's a classic." He put slices on plates and handed them to Amy and Nellie, along with napkins.

"Word," Nellie said, reaching for the red pepper flakes. "Nobody gets that about garlic salt. What do you like to cook?"

"Well, I started out with Egyptian food," he said, "because of my grandmother. My parents are Egyptian, but they don't cook. She really taught me. Now that I live on my own, I've branched out. I just took a Vietnamese cooking class, and it was awesome."

Nellie dropped her pizza. "Shut up! Vietnamese is my favorite!"

Dan kicked her. They'd come to find out if Sammy had betrayed them. If Nellie started talking about cooking, they'd never be able to get a word in edgewise.

She picked a piece of cheese off her pizza and ate

it while gazing into Sammy's dark eyes. Dan was surprised Sammy didn't burst into flame. His pizza stayed in the air, inches from his mouth, as he gazed back at Nellie. Seconds passed.

Dan kicked her harder.

"Actually," Nellie said, "there's a reason we're here. We wanted to ask you some questions."

"Fire away," Sammy said. His smile was so open and amiable that Dan hoped Amy was wrong. Sammy couldn't possibly have passed along the serum to an outsider.

"Sammy," Dan said, "do you remember that favor you did for me last year?"

"Sure," Sammy said. "I mixed up a little potion for you."

"When I contacted you, you said you would keep the secret."

Sammy looked uncomfortable. Dan's heart began to beat faster.

"We need to know exactly what happened," Amy said.

Sammy seemed to swallow his bite of pizza with an effort. He wiped his mouth hard with a napkin. "The thing is, I'm a scientist. And the number one quality you need to be a scientist is curiosity."

Dan's voice came out hoarse. "What did you do?"

"I work with substances that have to be disposed of according to regulations," Sammy said. He pointed to a red box sitting on the counter that said HAZARDOUS WASTE. "One sink is for washing up. One sink is for chemicals. There is a trap in the sink that I empty into the container."

Dan sank back. The one bite of pizza he'd taken rolled over in his stomach. "I poured the rest down the drain. . . ."

"Into the trap," Sammy said. "So I had a tiny bit. A residue. But it was enough."

"Enough for what?" Amy asked sharply.

"To experiment on."

Nellie let out a breath she'd been holding. "Oh, no."

"I'm a Cahill on both sides," Sammy said. "My mother is a Lucian, my father is an Ekat. My father was part of the leadership circle before he quit. He knew about the serum, and he told me about it, too. So when Dan Cahill walked into my lab . . . I couldn't help but be curious."

"You *replicated the serum*?" Amy asked. "Do you realize how dangerous that was?"

Sammy held up two hands. His eyes pleaded with them. "I know! I was very careful! I know I shouldn't have done it! But this is supposed to be the most powerful substance in the history of humanity. So I couldn't resist just running a few simple tests. I mean, think about it. How does the human mind really work? Is it biology and chemistry or some hybrid we haven't even *named* yet? The serum itself brings up so many fascinating questions."

"It does," Nellie said. "It totally does." She cleared her throat. "But those aren't questions you were allowed to be, um, asking."

"Those are questions that, if we could answer them, could benefit *everyone*," Sammy declared, leaning forward intently. "And the more I thought about it, the more I thought about all those Cahill legends about the physical strength of the Tomas, and the way the Lucian mind works . . . and how these serum strains entwine with DNA . . . and I thought, okay, if I just run a few experiments, maybe I can find some *good* from this crazy serum. What if certain parts could be recalibrated and I could lessen the side effects, boost the separate elements, and *customize* it for whatever the person taking it would want or need? What if I could eliminate the DNA factor? Just make it a kind of *medicine*? Just as an experiment," he added quickly. "Think about it. There have been *massive* leaps in the field of biochemistry since Gideon Cahill's time. If he knew what we know, what would he have crafted? How could he have made it safer? What could he have *cured*?"

"You *can't* make it safe," Amy said. "That's the whole point. It's a destructive power! It can lead to . . . terrible things."

"I know that," Sammy said quickly. "That's why I closed down the research."

Amy sagged in relief. "You did?"

"I realized pretty quickly that I was heading down a

dangerous path. If we're able to artificially boost things like physical prowess, creativity, the part of the brain that controls strategy and analysis . . . well, who would control it? Who would decide who gets what strain? There are some things that are better not invented. I mean, that kind of goes against the Ekat philosophy, but my mama raised me right."

"Sammy, we believe that you didn't mean any harm," Amy said. "But is there any way someone else could have gotten their hands on your experiments?"

"Of course not!" Sammy exclaimed. "I know how sensitive this is. My notes were coded and behind a firewall while I did the experiments, and then I wiped them when I was done. The lab is always locked. And I always destroy whatever serum I've made." He looked at each of their faces. "Anyway, Gideon's original formula? It's basically a death sentence."

"A death sentence?" Amy asked. "We knew it was dangerous, but . . ."

"It's the way it reacts with the human nervous system," Sammy said. "It shuts it down. It would take about a week and then . . ."

"So, with these experiments, what exactly did you find?" Nellie asked.

"I experimented with tiny doses in a variety of fillers," Sammy said. "Now we have centrifuges, automated analyzers . . . machines and procedures that Gideon couldn't even dream of. I basically altered the formula in a sophisticated way."

"You *altered* the formula?"

"Well, the first job was to make it less toxic. I was able to do that."

"So *your* version isn't a death sentence?"

"I don't think so—but I can't say there wouldn't be side effects. There'd be no way to really know without animal testing, and I'm not going to do that. I *was* able to do some rudimentary boosting of the separate traits and then get it down to a daily dose—a small trace element of serum suspended in a liquid—fruit juice worked well. I even made four formula strains for each branch: Lucian, Ekat, Tomas, Janus. The next step would have been figuring out exactly how to combine them in different strengths."

"Are you sure that you told no one?" Nellie asked.

"I'm positive," Sammy said.

Dan closed his eyes. Relief flooded him. The leak hadn't come from him.

Amy picked up her slice of pizza.

"Except for Fiske, of course," Sammy said. "And he was fine when I said I didn't feel comfortable doing any more work on it. He agreed."

Amy dropped the pizza. *"What?"*

"You mean *our* Fiske?" Dan blurted.

Sammy nodded. "Your Uncle Fiske. Tall guy, black jeans, silver hair? I recognized him from my dad's description. He came to see me, oh, about five or six months ago? He said Dan had told him about fabricating the serum, and he guessed that I had figured it out.

I told him about the experiments. So he asked for all my notes and said that they belonged in the Madrigal archive."

"What Madrigal archive?" Amy asked. "Do you know about this, Nellie? Dan?"

They both shook their heads.

Dan swallowed. "What . . . month did you meet him?"

"October."

"Fiske was in rehab the entire month of October," Amy whispered.

Sammy's voice shook. "Are you telling me that the man I spoke to *wasn't Fiske Cahill*?"

"I doubt it," Dan said. He felt sick.

"But he knew so much about the Cahills." Sammy looked pale.

Amy looked at her watch and jumped up. "We've got to talk to Fiske. Right now!"

CHAPTER 10

The Callender Institute was on the Upper East Side of Manhattan near the river, in a quiet neighborhood of town houses and amber streetlamps. It was like going back in time. Nellie cruised by, looking for a parking space, but couldn't find one. Finally, she pulled into a driveway, right in front of a DON'T EVEN THINK ABOUT PARKING HERE sign.

"I bet James Bond never worries about parking," she said.

They walked into the institute. It was set up like a private home, with thick multicolored carpets on the polished wood floors and seascapes on the walls. Shaded lamps discreetly lit a polished mahogany desk, behind which sat an older woman in a navy dress.

"We'd like to see our uncle, Fiske Cahill," Amy said.

"As you know, we don't have visiting hours per se at the institute," the woman said politely. "But we don't allow visitors after ten o'clock."

"It's very important that we see him," Nellie said. "And we know he's a night owl."

The woman smiled at them in a patronizing way. "I'm sure whatever you have to tell your uncle can wait until morning."

"Actually, it can't," Dan said. He threw a *we don't have time for this* look at Amy and simply walked by the woman. Amy followed.

The woman reached for the phone. Nellie put her hand over it, preventing her from picking it up.

"I'd think very carefully about that," she said sweetly. "You have a choice here. You can seriously jeopardize the plans for the Grace Cahill wing that is scheduled to open in two years. Or you can look the other way for exactly five minutes."

They locked eyes. "I think I'll read my magazine," the woman said.

"That's just what I was thinking," Nellie said. With a flourish, she sat on a tufted armchair to wait.

"There is a Madrigal archive," Fiske said. "But I've never met Sammy Mourad. And I've never been to the Columbia campus."

They had found their great-uncle reading in bed in a pool of soft yellow lamplight, his glasses pushed down on his nose. He had frowned deeply while they told him their story, and Amy had been shocked at how much older he looked. His skin was sallow and pale, and the lines around his mouth looked deeper.

Fiske had always been wiry and strong, but after undergoing physical therapy for a bad hip, he had grown weaker over the fall. Then winter had brought robust health. They'd uncrossed their fingers when he returned to his tae kwon do classes and began to paint and cook again. But then he had fallen ill again in March. Now he looked old and tired. Amy felt fear clutch at her heart. She placed her hand over his where it rested on the blanket.

"Are you feeling okay, Uncle Fiske?" Amy asked.

"Just fine." His smile was reassuring, but Amy noticed how his hand trembled as he picked up his water glass. "Dr. Callendar says the physical therapy has been very beneficial. I think I'll be home next week." He took a sip of water. "We need to get to the bottom of this. We should inform all the Madrigals, call in a team. . . ."

Amy shook her head. "Not yet."

"If not now, when?" Fiske frowned at her. "You think this person has taken the serum. This could have dire consequences for the *world*, Amy. Not to mention that you and Dan are now a target."

Amy looked at him, surprised. He held up a hand. "Yes, Nellie told me. As she should have. Don't treat me like an invalid. If what Sammy said is true, that means that Pierce could be taking a daily, weaker dose of the serum, but it has a cumulative effect. Every day, he gets stronger. We have to find a way to get the serum back . . . *without anyone knowing what it is and what it means.* This is the worst thing that could have happened."

Dan faded back in the room, his face in shadow. Fiske glanced over at him.

"And it's nobody's fault," he said firmly. "Not Sammy's, not Dan's, not anybody's. We have a very clever adversary. *We must stop J. Rutherford Pierce.*"

"We won't be able to stop him unless we find out more about him," Amy said. "If we surround ourselves with people, they'll just become targets, too. Right now he only knows me and Dan, and he wants to stop us."

Fiske looked at Amy over his eyeglasses. "He wants to *kill* you."

"That's our risk to take," Amy said. "I can't ask others to sacrifice their safety. Not after . . . after . . ." Her voice thickened, and she stopped.

Fiske looked down at Amy's hand on his arm. There was a long silence.

"Amy," he said with great gentleness, "it is a source of terrible sorrow to me, as it was to your grandmother, that you were thrust into all this. If I could go back and give you and Dan a normal life, if I could give my *own* life for that, I would. But you are what you are. You are a Cahill, the *head* of the Cahills. And you will not achieve peace with that until you understand something." He squeezed her hand and looked at her hard. "This is your life now. You can do your best, but you cannot protect everyone you love. You are not responsible for all the lives around you. You are only responsible for your own right action."

"I *have* to protect them," Amy said. "As head of the family, I *must*."

"To the best of your power, yes. But that doesn't mean excluding them from helping you!"

Amy set her jaw stubbornly. "Not yet," she said.

Dan's gaze went back and forth between Fiske and Amy, the battle of two strong wills.

"All right," Fiske said. "Then you have to leave the country. Tonight."

"What?" Dan asked. "That seems extreme."

"No. It's the only way." Fiske sat up straighter. "There's something I've been waiting to tell you. Mr. McIntyre had a will."

"I know," Amy said. "He left everything to Henry Smood."

"Not everything. Grace left him a house in Ireland. She wanted him to keep it ready for you. It's called Bhaile Anois, and now it's yours. That's where you must go."

Amy frowned. "How can we fight Pierce if we're in Ireland?"

"You don't know what you're fighting yet," Fiske said urgently. "You need time to dig, investigate . . . plan. The computer system is down. You can't do much here anyway. And you must trust Grace. Her instructions were very clear. When you had nowhere else to turn, you had to go there."

"But—"

Fiske interrupted Amy's objection. For a moment he looked like the old Fiske—fierce, powerful, ready to spring. "As soon as we're sure the system is bug-free, you'll get back on the network. You can do it just as easily from Ireland as you can from Attleboro."

Amy nodded slowly. She had to admit that was true.

Fiske leaned forward. "I'm glad you agree. There's a private plane waiting for you at Teterboro Airport in New Jersey."

Slowly, Amy smiled. "As usual, you're way ahead of me."

"Just one small step."

"But what about you?" Dan asked, moving forward out of the shadow. "We don't want to leave you here."

"This is the safest place I can be," Fiske said. "This is a world-renowned medical facility. Anyway, nobody's after me. They're after you." He turned to Amy. "Dan is the only one now who knows the serum formula. And where Dan is, you are."

Amy and Dan exchanged a glance. "All right," she said. "We hate to leave you. . . ."

"We'll be together again," Fiske promised. "Until then, stay safe."

When they reached the reception room, Nellie had gone. The woman in the navy dress looked up.

"She ran out," she said with an air of satisfaction. "I think you're being towed."

Amy and Dan pushed through the front door. Nellie was running down the street after a tow truck.

"Nellie!" Dan called.

But his voice was drowned out as a black car squealed to a stop at the curb. Two men got out. One of them flashed a badge.

"Federal agents. You're under arrest."

CHAPTER 11

They didn't have much time to think. Nellie had dashed around the corner after the tow truck.

If we go with them, Mr. Smood can get us out in a matter of hours, Amy thought. *If we fight, we'll get locked up.*

Even as she thought this, the agents were hustling them into the backseat of the black car. Amy slid over to make way for Dan.

The two agents sat in the front of the car. Amy looked at the door. There were no door handles. The car took off.

"What's the charge?" Amy asked.

There was no answer.

She leaned forward. "Can I call my attorney?"

No answer.

She took out her phone. No service.

"There must be a blocking device in the car," Dan whispered.

Where would they be going? Amy wondered. Most of the federal offices were downtown. But to her surprise they drove west through Central Park and then turned north toward the Bronx.

She and Dan exchanged glances. Something didn't feel right.

Amsterdam Avenue was quiet. It was past one in the morning now. Some people were on the streets, walking quickly, shoulders hunched against the chill. A group of young men exited a bar, laughing loudly. A shopkeeper walked out and straightened the stacks of papers outside his market. It seemed so strange to see street life go on when they were traveling . . . where? Amy felt the door with her fingers, searching for a latch, or a way to open the window. There was nothing.

The car moved through unfamiliar streets, making several turns. Now it cruised alongside an overgrown park. Amy glimpsed a tower in the distance. The area was deserted. Amy's blood turned cold. It seemed incredible that they were still in Manhattan, and there wasn't a soul around.

"I say, as soon as they open the door, we run for it," Dan murmured.

The car pulled over and stopped. Amy's heart was now hammering so hard against her ribs it hurt. She held on to the car seat, ready to spring. The two agents in the front got out.

Both doors opened simultaneously. They had no chance to run. They were grabbed roughly and pulled from the car. Amy's arms were pinned next to her sides and her wrists held together behind her back.

They were forced to march on a wide pedestrian walkway bordered by shrubs. They passed through a brick plaza and she saw a towering arched bridge off to her right. It was high and graceful, half steel, half stone. There were no car lights on it. It spanned the river and the highway.

She was marched through the park. The grip on her wrists was so tight she could almost feel the slender bones crunch. She could hear Dan's breathing behind her.

She still hadn't seen their faces. But as they passed under a streetlight, she caught sight of the agent's profile.

It was the smiling man from the cemetery.

Fear chilled her. Though she kept her head level, her eyes darted around, searching for an escape. The narrow path was surrounded by steep slopes tangled with brush. She strained her ears, but all she heard was a faint hum of traffic from far away.

They were shoved roughly down a steep stairway. The tower loomed above. Through the gloom she was just able to make out a sign.

Amy felt sweat dampen the small of her back. She was suddenly aware of everything—the coolness of the breeze, the shape of the leaves, the heavy sound of her guard's footsteps. She tried to think of a way to get away, but the grip was merciless and she couldn't leave Dan. He was being pulled so fast his feet dragged on the pavement. Her throat closed up. Her guard pushed her roughly forward.

The path turned, and she saw the bridge like a strange apparition. Half a steel span, half stone arches, it rose hundreds of feet above the Harlem River and the highways next to it. She knew that was where they were heading.

Two massive black metal doors guarded the bridge. They were splashed with graffiti and padlocked together, a heavy chain looped through the handles. The sign read ENTRY PROHIBITED. She felt a momentary relief, but it ended when her guard used his other hand to rip the chain from the door. She didn't have time to register the shock of that before she was pushed through and onto the bridge.

She heard the doors clang shut behind her. Pushing and pulling them now, the men forced them forward.

Under other circumstances, she would have noted that the view was breathtaking. The lights of Manhattan were tossed across the velvet night. The highways were ribbons of light.

"You've got a choice." The voice was low at her ear. After all that exertion, he wasn't even breathing hard.

"You can go over and land in the river, or the highway. The river is gonna feel like concrete anyway."

The other one snorted a laugh. He was short and muscular, with a blond buzz cut. "You see how nice we are? We're letting you choose."

She saw Dan's chin shaking. Then he gritted his teeth. "A couple of choirboys," he forced out.

Amy wanted so badly to reach out to him, grip his hand.

"Yeah, squirt," the shorter man holding Dan said. "And you're a couple of daredevils, horsing around on the bridge. I can see the headline now."

"Choose, or we'll choose for you." The man holding her wrists grinned. Amy saw the flash of perfect white teeth. She saw him up close, the texture of his pores, the shape of his eyebrows, his ears. He was someone she wouldn't look twice at on the street. Someone in line for coffee, or waiting for a bus, or taking his dog for a walk. What kind of a person, she thought, would throw two children off a bridge like it was all in a day's work?

They dragged them to the railing. The river was a dark oily channel. The streak of car lights on the road, the lights of the low buildings, the faint sound of a car horn—Amy heard it all with the same strange clarity. Her teeth were chattering. She looked straight up at the luminous sky.

"River," she said.

They released their wrists. She grabbed Dan's hand at last. She felt the texture of his skin, his slight fingers. The feel of them made tears sting her eyes. Her baby brother. She couldn't save him, couldn't protect him. . . . She had spent months and months running, training, lifting weights, and studying martial arts. And here they were, on this high bridge, with nowhere to turn. They wouldn't jump without a fight, but she knew they'd lose. They'd be thrown off if they didn't jump. She'd rather be thrown. She'd rather go down fighting.

The railing was only waist-high. She felt Dan's hand, tight in hers. She knew he was waiting for her signal.

"C'mon, kiddies, we don't have all day. Climb over the fence."

The metal railing was wet and cold. Amy curved her fingers around it. She put her hand over Dan's. Ears straining, she thought she heard the noise of a car. But it was coming from the direction of the pedestrian walkway.

"Get going!" the man behind her barked. He put his hands on her waist and pushed her roughly up. Amy felt her balance wobble as she hung on to the railing. Panic roared through her as she started to tip over into space.

"Amy!" Dan screamed.

The man tried to tear her hands away from the rail. She didn't have time to turn and fight, and her balance was off. She couldn't breathe as he squeezed her around the waist as she kicked, trying to push off the metal railing and send him off balance. It was like trying to unbalance a mountain.

The car engine noise turned from distant to near, and suddenly headlights raked across the bridge. A truck was barreling toward them. A tow truck with a yellow Jeep wheeling crazily behind it.

She had barely registered her shock when she was suddenly flipped over the railing. Amy screamed as the dark river rose up below her. She heard Dan screaming, the squeal of brakes. . . .

And someone had her by the ankle.

Dan's face, looking down at her, his mouth open, his eyes wild with terror. He had both hands wrapped around her ankle while the goon behind him had his arm wrapped around Dan's neck. Dan's face was purple.

Screaming, Amy swung in midair.

The black river so far below. Glints of reflected red on its surface. Her own heartbeat in her ears, roaring. . . .

Dan's grip loosened. He was losing air, losing her, she was losing, they were losing. . . .

The steel arch of the bridge, if she could just . . . manage . . . to grab that pipe that looped around the railing . . . Dan's grip loosened again, and she screamed as the river rushed up, but the momentum caused her to swing just a bit.

One . . . more . . . chance . . .

She had taken several classes in trapeze — a birthday gift from Fiske — and her muscle memory told her what to do: use the swing, get that arm extended, fingers straight out, ready to grab —

The noise of screeching metal assaulted her ears, blocking out the sound of her quick, hard breathing and the faint noise of traffic. Her fingers hit the pipe just as Dan let go and she was able to hold tight. The force of her body falling almost jerked her hand off the pipe, but she held on. She was now swinging above the river, holding on with only one hand. Her arm felt as though it was being ripped out of its socket.

Terror shimmered out through her fingers. She brought her other arm up and grabbed the pipe. She would not waste her energy and give in to the scream in her throat. She bit her lip and lifted her weight up, her arm muscles shaking with the effort.

She landed over the pipe on her stomach and was able to take one shuddering breath before sliding, inch by agonizing inch, closer to the bridge. Her hands smacked against the ledge and she allowed herself one sob of relief as she pulled herself up to the top of the railing.

As she yanked herself up, she saw the fishtailing Jeep hit both men. They went flying. Even from here, she heard the crack of skull against pavement.

Dan's hands were underneath her armpits, dragging her over, and that was a good thing, because now her legs weren't working. Dan's body shuddered with sobs. Together they toppled onto the walkway. His tears mixed with the sweat on her face.

"I let you go! I thought you fell!"

"No . . . I made it. I made it." Amy tasted blood in her mouth and realized she'd bitten through the skin on her lip. Over Dan's shoulder she saw the tow truck parked at a crazy angle. One of the men was struggling to his knees, shaking his head to clear it. Nellie's head stuck out.

"GET IN!" she screamed.

Dan pulled Amy to her feet, and they ran. Nellie flung open the door and they jumped into the cab of the truck. She floored it.

"What's at the end of this bridge?" she shouted.

"I don't know!" Amy yelled. "But it's probably the same kind of metal doors as the other side. They have a chain and a padlock!"

"Not tonight they don't. This baby is built like a tank. Buckle up and hang on!"

They were screaming down the bridge now, the speedometer needle rising higher. The two black metal doors loomed ahead. Amy knew they were firmly locked, and that they were padlocked on the other side with a thick metal chain.

"Hang on!" The truck hit the gate with a crash and Nellie kept her foot on the gas. The jolt sent them all flying forward, straining against their seat belts.

The truck didn't crash through. Metal screamed as it only slammed the two doors open a few feet apart. They were wedged halfway through, trapped between them. The chain kept the two doors linked.

Nellie stared ahead. "Well. That *almost* worked." She glanced behind. "And we're about to have company."

Amy twisted and looked back. The two men were racing down the bridge toward them.

"Climb out the windows and over the hood," Nellie ordered.

Nellie wriggled out her open window, squeezed through the opening between the truck and the metal doors, and yelled, "Tomorrow, I'm going on a diet!" as she scrambled onto the hood. Amy and Dan followed. They slid down the hood and jumped off, now safe on the pavement and facing a dark, hilly park. With a quick glance behind, they saw the men leap onto the back of the tow truck and clamber over the top.

"Run," Nellie ordered unnecessarily.

The path twisted steeply uphill. They pounded up a set of stone stairs. Winded, they paused at the top, and saw below the two men still racing down their path, their legs as powerful and regular as pistons in an engine. They started to run again, streaking through the pathways. If they kept going up, they hoped to reach a road eventually. Amy felt her breath hot and rasping in her chest. Her lungs were giving out. The fight to get back on the bridge had taken most of her strength.

Finally, they spilled out onto a dark, empty street. Amy almost sobbed with disappointment. There was no one around. The stores were closed, the metal gates locked.

A car cruised through a red light and turned down the street. One of the men vaulted the stone wall. Nellie ran into the middle of the street as the car zoomed toward her. She did not move. She closed her eyes.

With a squeal of brakes, it stopped only inches from her.

A head popped out of the window. Amy couldn't hear the words, but she got the general sense of outrage, alarm, and irritation. She and Dan ran toward the car as Nellie slid onto the hood and crossed her arms.

"Are you crazy, lady?" The African-American man was white-haired and angry. "I'm on my way to work! Don't give me a hard time now."

"I just need a ride," Nellie said. "Me and my friends."

"Do I look like a *bus*?"

The two men were now on the sidewalk, watching. Amy knew it wouldn't take long before they would make a decision. With the same chilling neutrality, they could kill the man in the car, too.

She ran over, already reaching for the cash in her belt. She handed the man a hundred-dollar bill. "Here's your fare."

He stared at it. "I think I just started a business. Ernie's Car Service. Get in."

They hopped in the backseat and Ernie took off. It took whole minutes for their heartbeats to slow.

"Nice rescue," Dan said. "How'd you get that truck?"

"They shouldn't have stopped for coffee," Nellie said, and winked.

CHAPTER 12

Ernie was heading to his job at a downtown bakery, and he obligingly dropped them off on the Upper West Side.

Nellie had contacted Fiske from the car, and to her great relief a black late-model car was waiting at the corner of Broadway and 110th. They stood for a minute, shivering in the suddenly cold wind. A pattering of rain hit the streets.

"Here we go, kiddos," Nellie said. "After tonight, I think you'll be safer in Ireland."

"There's one thing," Amy said. "Those goons — do you think there was something crazy about how strong they were?"

"What do you mean?" Nellie asked.

"One of them ripped the chain link from the door with one hand," Amy said. "And the way they ran . . . how fast they caught up to us."

"They never broke a sweat," Dan said. "And you'd just hit them with a car."

"Do you think . . ." Nellie left the sentence unfinished.

"I don't know," Amy said. "Could Pierce have used Sammy's experiments to give his guards a boost?"

"I think he's capable of anything," Nellie said. "We saw that tonight."

"That means we're up against a bunch of serum-boosted guys?" Dan asked.

Nellie felt hopelessness suddenly engulf them, as relentless as the rain sweeping up Broadway.

"We'll beat them," Amy said. "We'll beat them because we have to."

Nellie smiled. Leave it to Amy to sum it up. Simple and clear.

Nellie wanted to burst out crying. She wanted to tell them how proud she was of them.

Instead, she had to let them go on alone.

"The car will take you to Teterboro Airport in New Jersey," she told them. "There's a private jet waiting there under the name Swift. When you land in Dublin, someone on that end will meet you." She hugged them both. "Good luck, kiddos. Remember — minimal contact from now on, but always let me know where you are. Keep a low profile. As soon as Pony gets the system back up, we'll figure this all out. And we'll beat them."

"Because we have to," the three of them said.

Nellie ran across deserted Broadway against the light. She hadn't wanted Amy and Dan to know where she was going, because they would have insisted on coming, too. Tonight it had been brutally brought home to her that Pierce would stop at nothing to get at anyone with access to the serum. He was willing to throw two kids off a bridge — *her* two kids.

They'd survived, but the terror they'd felt tonight would haunt them. Nellie touched her shoulder. The scar from the gunshot wound was still red. She'd been a hostage. She knew about nightmares.

There was one more target. One that had occurred to her in Ernie's car. The only other person who knew the serum formula.

They never should have left Sammy alone.

Sammy had mentioned that he was going to pull an all-nighter. With any luck, he'd still be there, safe and sound and all nerdy and adorable in his lab. Nellie tried to text and run at the same time as she headed toward the chemistry building.

```
ARE YOU STILL THERE
SAMMY IT'S NELLIE
```

No answer.

When she reached the chemistry building, the security guard wouldn't let her up and wouldn't confirm if Sammy had left.

"But I was just here!" Nellie protested. "I brought him a pizza."

A young man was signing out as she was talking. "Are you a friend of Sammy's? I'm his roommate, Josh."

"Yes! Is he still here?"

"He left about a half hour ago," Josh said. "There was some kind of family emergency. They called up for Sammy—his uncle was here."

Nellie shifted her feet. "His uncle?"

"Yeah. I was worried, so after a minute I came down after him. I saw him standing with a couple of guys by the curb. They were talking to him, and then suddenly he just kind of collapsed. It must have been seriously bad news. They helped him into the car. Jeez, I hope his family is okay. I've been texting him, but he hasn't answered."

Nellie swallowed against the ball of fear in her throat. "Did you notice anything about the car?"

"It was a black SUV. I don't know what the make was. I don't pay attention to cars."

"Anything at all . . ."

"First state."

Nellie shook her head, confused.

"The license plate said 'the first state.' I noticed that because I didn't know there *was* a first state. Hey, if you track him down, will you tell him to give me a buzz?"

Nellie thanked him and walked a few feet away.

She whipped out her phone and activated her search engine. She typed in *first state*.

Delaware was the first state to ratify the US Constitution. "First state" was on its license plate.

"Delaware," Nellie muttered. "That really narrows it down."

CHAPTER 13

Dublin, Ireland

They arrived in Dublin in a hard rain. All they saw was a curtain of gray. They made it through customs quickly and walked into the lounge. A young man with a dark wool cap pulled down to his eyebrows stood.

"Sarah and Jack Swift?" he asked in a thick Irish brogue. At Amy's nod, he added, "Guess you landed at last."

Amy and Dan looked at him, confused. Their plane had been early.

"The birds," he said. "Swifts. Legend is that they spend their lives in the air and never land. Ach, never mind. Welcome to Ireland. I'm Declan. Follow me."

They followed him out to a parking lot, where a battered truck waited.

"This is some rain," Dan said.

"We call it a little mist here." Declan climbed behind the steering wheel. "You can sit in the back, there's a blanket there — heating's not the best in this heap. It's a long drive. There are sandwiches and a thermos of tea in the basket for your dinner. We won't be stopping."

"All right," Amy said. "What's the name of the town?"

"Meenalappa. Don't get excited, there's not much to it."

"How many hours is the drive?"

"As many as it takes, I'd guess."

Declan turned on the engine and drove. Soon they were on a highway, and Amy and Dan lost track of where they were going or why as the numbing monotony of a drive in the rain took over.

Amy had fallen into an exhausted sleep on the plane, and now she was wide awake. She wished she could fall into that dark oblivion again. Because for the first time since she'd stood over an open grave only twenty-four hours ago, she had time to think about the last time she saw Jake.

She and Dan and Fiske had flown to Rome for New Year's. Somehow, away from Attleboro, away from all those reminders of Evan and what she'd lost, Amy had felt herself come back to life again. She still remembered the New Year's Eve dinner that Jake had cooked for all of them. Atticus had woven tiny fairy lights all over the dark, somber apartment until it glowed with cheer. She remembered the sudden, surprising snowfall that began as they ate their dessert, and how Jake had grabbed her hand and said, "Let's walk." That midnight walk through the snow had given her a glimpse of a new life, a new way of being. An Amy who wasn't tortured by memory and crushed by guilt.

She stared out at the cold gray rain, wondering how a memory that had once given her hope could hurt her heart so much.

She had sent a text to Jake as she waited on the runway in New Jersey.

HAVE TO GO AWAY FOR A WHILE. NO
INTERNET. I WILL BE IN TOUCH.

She had added I LOVE YOU and taken it out. How could she sign off that way, when she could be going away for a long time? How dare she use the word *love* when she never knew, from one day to the next, what her life would be? She was midair, like a swift, never able to land.

Darkness fell, and the sound of rain drumming on the roof lulled them into a doze. When they woke they were off the highway and driving on a series of small lanes. They could smell the sea. Declan drove faster than Amy would like, since she couldn't see beyond the headlights. But he seemed to know every twist and curve.

The car climbed a small rise and then made an

abrupt turn into what seemed to be a row of bushes. The opening was barely wide enough for the car.

Through the rain they glimpsed a whitewashed cottage, long and low. Declan pulled up and cut the engine. Without a word, he slid out of the front seat and clomped away.

"Are we supposed to follow him?" Dan asked.

"I guess so."

They headed out into the rain. Declan had swung open the front door, and he turned and handed Amy a key.

"My sister came out earlier and put on the heat and stocked the cupboards. There's everything you need inside. Bicycles in the garage. It's about a fifteen-minute ride to the village."

He headed back toward the car.

"Which way?" Amy called after him.

He gestured, but it was hard through the rain to see if he meant left or right. He hopped back into the car and drove out.

"Ah, it's that legendary Irish charm I've heard so much about," said Dan.

They walked inside. Declan had switched on the lamps, and the room looked bright and welcoming. There was a small fireplace with two plump sofas in front of it. Amy peeked into the next room, a large kitchen with another fireplace. The back staircase led to the bedrooms, all made up with fresh linens. Laid out on the sinks were new toothbrushes, toothpaste, and soaps.

The rain lashed the dark panes. They didn't know where they were, or why they were here, or what they would do the next day. They were too exhausted to care. They slipped into sheets that smelled softly of lavender and reminded them of Grace, finally feeling safe enough to sleep.

When Amy awoke, the sky was blue outside her window. She peeked into Dan's room but the bed was empty. She glanced out the back window. A sloping lawn behind the cottage led to a dock with a motorboat tied to the piling. The inlet snaked out toward a misty blue bay.

Dan stood on the lawn, his back to her. He was dressed but barefoot, the wind ruffling his hair.

She started to turn away, but stopped. There was something so . . . solitary and sad about the scene. Something about his posture, the way his hands hung at his sides, told her that he was hurting.

She shoved her feet inside her sneakers, went down the back stairs, and pushed open the kitchen door. The scent of fresh meadow and salty sea hit her nostrils as she climbed a rise to stand next to Dan.

"Did you notice that the house is in a hollow?" Dan

asked without turning to greet her. "And it's invisible from the road. We have three exit points—the road, the sea, and across the field. This is Grace's safe house."

"I hadn't thought of it that way." And it hurt to see that her little brother had figured it out. He should be pitching baseballs, not noticing escape routes.

Dan stared with a fierce gaze at the inlet. His chin trembled. "I let go," he said. "On the bridge. I had you, and I let go."

"You *saved* me," Amy said quietly. "You caught me as I went over. And you held on while some goon was *strangling* you."

"Amy . . ." Dan turned to her. His face was anguished. "I felt you *slipping*. I had you, and then I couldn't hold on. I couldn't hold on! I thought you were dead!"

"You *caught* me!" Amy cried. "You saved my life! And I'm here, Dan. I'm right here because of *you*."

"I'm the reason we had to run away," he said. "I was so stupid! I got us into this mess. I'm the reason Pierce has the serum. Now he's trying to kill us, and we probably have the FBI looking for us, too. I just messed up everywhere, big-time. I never get it right."

"You get it right plenty of the time," Amy said. "Maybe not *all* the time. But nobody does. Especially not me."

"I'll follow this through," Dan said. "I have to—I started it. We'll stop J. Rutherford Pierce together. But after that, I'm out."

"What do you mean, out?" Amy asked, startled.

Dan took a breath. "I don't want you to think this is one of my crazy impulsive decisions. I mean it. I don't want to be a Cahill anymore."

"You can't just . . . resign!"

"Fiske did. He left. He renounced the family. He disappeared, traveled all over the world. . . ."

"Fiske was an *adult* when he did that! You're only thirteen!" Amy shook her head. "Look, Dan. We've both felt like quitting plenty of times—we've scraped the very bottom. And we've always found a way to go on."

Dan's mouth was twisted with the effort not to cry. "This is *different*!"

"It's always different," Amy said soothingly. "But then we—"

"NO!" Dan shouted the word, and Amy's mouth snapped shut.

"No," he said, more quietly, and that stillness frightened her more than his outburst. "I haven't figured it all out yet. But I've been through enough. I've *done* enough to know this: I don't want to be a Cahill anymore. I don't want to live in Attleboro. I don't want any of it."

Amy felt his words like a knife in her heart. "You want to . . . leave me?"

"Of course not!" Dan slammed his hand against his leg in frustration. "I just . . . can't . . . live like this anymore. Maybe I can live with Nellie somewhere . . . for a while. Maybe Fiske will take off again and I can go with him. Not forever. You can keep training, and keep the Cahill network going, and keep staying alert for the next bad guy to come along. Because there'll always *be* another one. But I don't want to. I . . . *can't!*" The word was torn out of his throat. She saw his shoulders shaking. He held his head in both hands. "You don't know what it's like," he whispered. "To have the serum *in your head.*"

Amy opened her mouth, but nothing came out. Of course she didn't know. Couldn't know. What was she supposed to do? Yell at Dan? Plead with him? Tell him that he was abandoning her? When obviously this was the hardest decision he'd ever made?

Wasn't this what she wanted for him? Safety? A little bit of normal? No matter how much it cost her. No matter how much it hurt.

"Okay," she said. "We'll work it out. I won't stand in your way."

"You'll still be my sister. That won't change."

"I know."

They were silent for a while, listening to the wind in the grass. Amy felt turned inside out by Dan's pain. Her brother looked so young at that moment, standing in the grass barefoot, with his messy bed head. But his eyes looked older. Older than a thirteen-year-old's should look.

If he had to let go of her to have a normal life, the right thing, the brave thing, would be to let him go. But could she?

Clouds had covered the sun, and the inlet was now iron gray with flecks of white. Amy shivered.

If she let Dan go, she'd be alone.

After a hasty breakfast, they wheeled the bicycles out of the garage and headed for the lane.

"Left, or right?" Amy asked.

"I think I remember seeing the headlights turn right last night," Dan said.

"And it's downhill," Amy said. "Let's try it."

They pedaled for some minutes in silence. Soon they saw another bicyclist heading toward them.

"Excuse me, sir? Which way is the village?" Amy called.

"Not too far," he answered shortly, and pedaled quickly away.

They kept on pedaling. After a bit they saw a woman exit a cottage by the road and stop to water a pot full of bright red flowers.

"Excuse me, is this the way to the village?" Dan called.

"Sure, if you keep on, you'll hit something or other," the woman replied, and turned and walked quickly back into her house.

"Super McFriendly folks here in leprechaun land," Dan observed.

But after about ten minutes of riding, the road dipped and curved, and the village appeared, a cluster of houses and shops. They jumped off their bikes and leaned them against the side of a grocery with a bright blue door.

The bell jangled as they walked in. A young woman sat behind the counter, reading a book. She didn't look up.

Picking up a wicker basket, they filled it with food. They put the basket on the counter.

"It's a pretty village," Amy said. "Have you lived here long?"

"Long enough." She totaled up their purchases.

"Is there a good place to eat lunch nearby?" Dan asked.

"Folks say Sean Garvey's is good, but whether you'll think it is I can't predict," the girl said.

"Can we leave our groceries here for now?" Amy asked.

"Suppose you can."

"Nice to meet you, too," Dan said.

They walked out. Across the street they saw a sign for Sean Garvey's and swung open the door. The bar was crowded with locals, and they all fell silent as Amy and Dan walked in. A pretty waitress with reddish hair and hazel eyes led them to a table by the window and put two menus on the table.

"I'm starting to get the feeling I'm not wanted," Dan said.

"I guess they're not used to strangers," Amy said.

Dan studied the menu. "I think I'll skip the bangers and mash. I feel like I've been banged and mashed enough already."

They ordered sandwiches and observed the locals. Dan kept having an odd feeling, as though he was in a familiar place. He'd never been to this part of Ireland, or this village, yet he recognized something about it.

The waitress frowned as she folded napkins, and Dan felt a jolt.

She looks like Amy.

What was it? The way her mouth turned down? The shape of her face?

He looked back at Amy as she chewed her sandwich. Now she looked nothing like the waitress, really. He must be crazy.

After lunch they bought backpacks and spare clothes at a small store. Then they walked through the nearby churchyard. At least they didn't have to worry about people staring at them.

Dan paused to rest, leaning against a massive rock streaked with moss.

"Dan, what are you doing? It might be a gravestone."

"It's not a gravestone, it's just a rock." Dan stepped away and ran his hands along the stone. "See? No carvings." Just as he said that, his fingers traced a depression in the stone. He followed the line up, slightly down, up again, tracing a letter in the stone.

He scraped at the moss with a fingernail, clearing it away. "Amy . . . look at this."

She leaned down. "I don't see anything."

Dan continued to work at the stone, scraping off the moss. Then he stepped back and they caught their breath.

It was the Madrigal *M*.

CHAPTER 14

The girl was in the same position at the grocery, still reading a book.

"We were just walking in the churchyard," Amy said in a casual tone, "and we noticed this gigantic rock there."

"One of our more thrilling sights here in the village," the girl said. She flipped a page in her book.

"There's an *M* traced in the surface of the rock," Dan said. "And it looks really ancient."

"It's just a rock," the girl said. "I doubt there's anything carved in it."

Dan knew the girl was lying by the way she turned a page of her book. She hadn't had time to read it. He held out the picture he'd taken on his phone. He'd snapped it and sent it to Nellie.

She flicked a quick glance at it. "I don't see anything. Let me get your groceries." She turned and leaned down to pick up the sack.

Dan gave Amy a sharp nudge. Tattooed on the small of the girl's back was clearly a Madrigal *M*.

Amy took the sack in her arms. "If it's just a rock," she said, "why is the same *M* tattooed on your back?"

For the first time, they saw emotion on the girl's face as her pale skin was splashed with pink.

"It's a symbol of the village," she said, lifting her chin and brushing a strand of dark hair out of her eyes. "Meenalappa."

"Then why didn't you say that about the rock?"

"Must I have chats about rocks with every eejit tourist that walks into my shop?" she asked defiantly. "Now get back to your tourist bus and kiss my Blarney Stone."

"We're not from a tourist bus," Dan said. "We're staying at a cottage nearby. Bhaile Anois."

The girl stared at them. Her gaze moved from Dan's face to Amy's and then back again. Then the tenseness left her body, and she smiled.

"That Declan. He's thick as a plank. You'd think your own brother would let you know who he drove to the cottage last night. I heard there was a tourist bus in the next village—they've a nice church there, it's on the tourist track. Sometimes the folks walk down here for lunch at the pub. Sorry to bite your heads off. We're very protective about our village, especially when there's people staying at Bhaile Anois."

"That's okay," Dan said. It was amazing how a grin transformed the girl's face.

"There's Cahill all over you," the girl said. "I should have seen it."

"We're Grace Cahill's grandchildren," Amy said.

"Dan and Amy, of course. Anyway," she said, "we have a saying in my house, and in the village. Anything for Grace. Now that includes you. Oh, where are my manners, I'm Fiona Kilhane. My grandmother was caretaker of the cottage—she was a good friend of Grace's. I'm sorry about her passing."

"Thank you," Amy said.

"Tell us about the rock," Dan said.

"It's almost as old as the village itself," Fiona said. "It goes beyond memory, back into folklore, I guess. The children of every generation tell the tales of the villager the rock commemorates. Hundreds and hundreds of years ago, she was born here. She went away for a long time and returned to have a daughter, only to go away again. The children call her a good witch. It's said that she protected the village from the plague, that she was a selkie from Atlantis, that she spun threads into gold. Her name was—"

"Olivia." Amy breathed the name.

"That's right," Fiona said. "Grace must have told you the legend. Many years later, her daughter returned here. She carved an *M* in the stone."

"Madrigal," Dan said.

"Oh, yes—that name has come down to us. We call it the Madrigal rock. It's a symbol of the village, I guess, our Madrigal."

Dan felt Amy's excitement match his. Fiona was talking about their ancestor Olivia Cahill. Her daughter Madeleine had been the first Madrigal.

This is our ancestral village, Dan thought. *This is where Olivia Cahill was born.*

Amy and Dan pedaled back to Bhaile Anois. Now the landscape looked fresh and meaningful to them. This is where they came from.

"Why an *M*, though?" Dan asked Amy.

"Because she couldn't put up a stone with her mother's name on it," Amy guessed. "It would have been too dangerous. Maybe the word *Madrigal* had a secret meaning to both of them."

They pushed through the tall hedge, and the white farmhouse sat snug and bright in its hollow. Dan felt Amy next to him, her hands resting lightly on the handlebars. She, too, was looking at the house. He knew that she was thinking the same thing. It was that mind-meld that happened with them so often.

"Grace had a reason she wanted us to come here," he said. "And it wasn't just protection."

"I know."

They wheeled the bikes into the garage and brought their bags into the house.

"Whenever we've needed her, she's been there," Amy said. "Even after she was gone. She gave us McIntyre and Fiske and Nellie. And now she's led us here."

"It's here," Dan said. "Whatever it is. There's something in the house."

They exchanged the briefest of glances, then sprang into action. Amy headed to the small study off the kitchen. She searched the desk and the bookshelves. She pressed against floorboards and tapped against walls.

Dan headed upstairs. He poked around the rooms, moving dressers and examining floorboards for a telltale loose board. He scrutinized the gray stone fireplace in the master bedroom where Amy had slept. He crawled over the floors of the remaining small, spare bedrooms. He knocked on their walls.

Finally, he climbed the winding wooden staircase to the attic bedroom, so small it had room only for a bed and a small table. One high round window gave a faint glimpse of blue sky. There was no closet, only a row of pegs along one wall.

Frustrated, he started down the stairs again. He hit the landing and made the turn, pounding down the remaining stairs.

He stopped.

He walked up the stairs again.

Then down.

Dan dropped to his knees. He examined every inch of the staircase, crawling up and down it. When he reached the bottom, he saw Amy standing in the hall, watching him.

"Yeah," he said. "I'm probably crazy. But there's something different about the sound of the stairs at the top from the bottom. It's just a little thing, but—"

He stopped. Amy had leaned right next to a candle sconce. It had a mirror backing, so that the candlelight would be caught and reflected. In that muddy reflection he'd seen it. The matching sconce on the other wall was slightly different. The metal scrollwork on the ledge was a different design. But in all other respects the sconces were a perfect pair.

He ran his fingers along the scrollwork. Carefully, he tugged on the sconce itself. It moved in his hand and he quickly tried to catch it. It hung steady, still anchored to the wall, but a few inches away. He pulled it all the way down, and the staircase rose into the air.

Beyond it was a secret room.

Dan walked up a few steps and peered in. Then he turned to Amy.

"After you," he said.

CHAPTER 15

Amy passed through the opening. She straightened and felt along the wall for a light switch. It turned on a pretty lamp with a blue glass shade that sat on a white table.

Dan followed. They were in a small, square room. The floorboards were painted white and the ceiling sky blue, perhaps to make up for the lack of windows. The room was tucked under the eaves. Amy guessed that it would be impossible to tell from outside the house that it existed.

Next to the white table was a wooden chair with a deep purple cushion on the seat. She could visualize Grace sitting in the chair with her straight-backed posture. There was a painting on one wall, and on the other an ornate gold mirror.

She walked closer to the table and leaned over to study the painting. The childlike forms depicted brightly colored woods and sky and a splash of yellow against a green field. She recognized it immediately. She had given it to Grace for her birthday when Amy was nine. She had worked on it so carefully—it was the view from Grace's window seat in the library. The place they used to curl up together with a pot of cocoa and a plate of cookies. She had painted it in spring, when the giant forsythia bush was blooming. Grace had called the bush "George" because she had buried a favorite goldfish there years before. "Oh, I see George is ready to bloom," she would say in early spring.

Dan walked over to a wooden filing cabinet next to the table. He opened the drawer and flicked through the files. Amy stood, looking over his shoulder. The files were marked by Grace's strong handwriting.

> *HOUSE ACCOUNTS*
> *Firewood Delivery*
> *Electric*
> *Trash Removal*
> *Phone*
> *Grocery Account*

Amy flipped through them. "These are duplicates," she said. "These files are all downstairs in the study."

"Why would Grace need two sets of files?" Dan wondered.

"Because these are a cover," she said. She began to remove the files, stacking them neatly on the desk.

Then she reached down into the drawer. With some tugging and pulling, she found that there was a panel on the bottom. She lifted it up, then withdrew a metal box.

"This is what we're meant to find," she said.

Dan studied the lock. "An alphabet combination lock. So we need a word, not numbers."

"Something only we would know," Amy said. She bit her lip. "Whenever Grace has left something she hopes we'll find, she also gives us a clue. There's got to be a clue in this room."

Dan looked around. "There's not much here to go on."

They went through the files carefully, but nothing leaped out at them. Then they examined the room, but it was as bare as it looked.

"There's got to be something," Amy said. Amy's gaze rested on the painting. The blob of yellow bush was painted so badly. It was nice of Grace to hang it. Especially when she'd done much better paintings than this one.

Something only we would know . . .

She returned to the box. She spun the letters.

G-E-O-R-G-E

The lid opened.

Amy lifted out a notebook, and underneath that, another box, this one wrapped in kitchen twine. Dan hovered over her shoulder as she untied it.

She opened the top of the box. Inside sat an old journal, a little bigger than a paperback. It was leather bound, and she could see the ruffled, yellowed pages on one side. "It looks ancient," she murmured.

"It *smells* ancient," Dan said.

It was true. It smelled like old paper, musty and dry, but something else . . . something medicinal. Amy opened it carefully. There must have been plants or herbs pressed in its pages at one time—she could see the ghostly traces they'd left on the yellowed pages. There were beautiful ink renderings of plants and leaves and flowers. Carefully turning the pages, she saw a recipe for a poultice against "the ague," the best method for bleaching stains out of muslin, a list of prices next to items like a bolt of linen, a cask of wine, tea. . . .

"It's a household account book," Amy said. "Definitely written by a woman. And a kind of diary. I mean, you can figure out her life by reading what she did every day. It looks like some of it is in Latin . . . or Italian? Both, I think."

"Who owned it?" Dan asked. "And why did Grace hide it?"

Amy turned back to the inside cover.

Olivia Behan Cahill
Household Book
Anno Domini 1499

A shiver ran down her spine. Dan let out a long exhalation.

"Whoa," he said. "It's Great-great-great-great et cetera grandma's book!"

Amy turned to the back cover of the book. In a strong clear hand, faded over time, was written: *Ret'd for safekeeping to the care of the village of Meenalappa. 1526 M.C.*

"Madeleine Cahill," Amy breathed. "She brought the book back to Meenalappa in 1526. After her mother died. And somehow it survived, all these years! Amazing." She carefully leafed through the pages. "Look, Dan—there is a gap here. Five pages completely inked out."

"Why would someone do that? To cover something up?"

"Maybe." The ink was dark and black, line after line bleeding into the next until it covered every bit of blank paper. There was something somber and chilling about it. Something that reminded her of the dark days she'd spent after the funerals of Evan, Alistair, Natalie. . . .

"Or maybe these pages are a memorial," Amy said slowly. "Remember the story? That Gideon was killed, and her four children scattered. . . . These five pages are her grief. And then look, she doesn't write anything until July 10, 1508. . . ." Amy counted on her fingers. "That could be the date of Madeleine's birth! Look, here she drew the Madrigal *M*."

She pointed to the oversized, hand-drawn *M* in the middle of a page adorned with flowers and leaves. Again there were recipes and medicines, lists of ingredients and amounts. . . .

"Look," Amy said. "She stops writing here — she has ten blank pages. And she's copied out a poem. Then here — she writes, *I miei viaggi*. 'My travels,'" Amy translated. "After that the rest of the book is written in code!"

"I'm guessing we're here to crack it," Dan said.

"Maybe Grace already did!"

Excited, Amy picked up Grace's notebook. Only about a third of the book was written in. There were lists of Latin words and translations of old Italian to modern Italian. Then there were notations that didn't make any sense at all.

"I think Grace tried to break the code, but wasn't able to," Amy said.

Dan groaned. "Why isn't it ever easy?"

As she flipped the pages, an envelope fell out.

Amy's heart fluttered. "It's from Grace," she said to Dan.

The note wasn't long.

> My dears, if you are here, you need to be here, and for that I am sorry. The worst has occurred. The secret we have guarded for centuries is out in the world, and you must stop it. Only you can.
>
> I think this book can help you. There is a way out of your difficulty. I was unable to find it. I ran out of time.
>
> This will be my last visit to the cottage. Enjoy your time here, no matter how brief. I am sorry to say that our struggle is never finished, only abandoned.
>
> I hope my love and trust in you is as clear to you today as it is to me as I write this. G.

"The secret is out in the world," Dan said. "The serum."

Amy touched the letter G, so bold, so strong. "She was afraid this day would come."

"Somewhere in there," Dan said, pointing to the

book, "is the answer to our problem. Grace gave us a way to fight J. Rutherford Pierce!"

By the evening, they had to give up. Olivia's book was a fascinating glimpse into life in Ireland in the early sixteenth century, but they couldn't see how what she wrote could help them. And they could not break the code.

"There's too much Latin and Italian," Dan said sleepily from his prone position on the floor. "And if I have to read one more poultice recipe, I'll tear my hair out." He raised himself on his elbows. "You know who we need to call. Atticus and Jake know these dead languages. They could—"

"No," Amy interrupted.

Dan sat upright. "While we're sitting here, Pierce is gaining power every day with the serum. We're the only ones who can stop him. We have to use everything we can, every*one* we can. You might want to protect everybody," he said. "I get that. But if the whole world falls apart, what good did it do?"

Amy jackknifed to her feet. "Let's just go to bed."

Dan's words pounded in Amy's head as she tucked the book under her arm and followed him up the worn wooden stairs to their rooms. She wanted to tell him he was wrong. She wanted to say, *You don't know what it's like to be in charge.* She wanted to fling an accusation at him — *You're the one who wants to run away! You don't get to have a vote anymore!* But she was too exhausted to fight.

She pulled on the sweats they'd bought in town, brushed her teeth, and turned out the light.

Sleep wouldn't come. She tossed and turned for an hour. When she closed her eyes, she felt herself falling, the dark, oily river rushing up at her. She felt Dan's fingers weakening. Panicked, she reached for the light. She propped herself up on pillows and picked up Olivia's book.

As she read, her eyebrows knit together. All these years, they'd wondered about the fascinating Gideon Cahill, the man who set out to stop a plague and developed a powerful serum. Who knew that his wife, Olivia, was just as fascinating and brilliant as he was? The journal made clear that it was Olivia who gathered the serum ingredients, Olivia who assisted Gideon in the lab, Olivia who kept the family together. Amy read Olivia's words.

The power he sought for healing transmogrified into a beast. A beast with the power of great destruction. And so it must itself be destroyed. To each is its opposite. The opposite negates the other.

She looked again to the poem right before the coded end of the book. She'd read it that evening several times, but hadn't understood it. She read it again, her heartbeat thudding in her ears.

Four souls, four elements, now dispersed.
'Twas as though my Family, cursed
and burdened — lo! to pass through years
of Strife, Calumny, Fears.
Yet beneath my beating Heart my Secret gave me
joy and hope —
a future seen — not grasped. My Joy, you have
strength enough to cope
and take up battle not with arms but wisdom
gained from ancient land
kept close and passed from hand to hand
to mio maestro di vita, thee of timeless woman,
universal man.
Then he to me bequeathed it, and with instruction
bid
and I, through his own methods, hid.
Using this, gathered I the parts. And with one
dram shall mend
what was torn asunder. And to the ash heap
send.
I take and here record from what my guide hath
guarded
with no edges glimpsed, dark sketched the key
imparted.
My Joy, my Song, you have my charge. Now take
what thee owns outright, count eight and on
the sixth do pause.
Take that sixth, match to first that Romans
brought, and end assault on Nature's Laws.

Four souls, four elements. It was clear to Amy what Olivia meant. The four souls were the children: Luke, Thomas, Katherine, Jane.

Four elements: the four parts of the serum.

Dispersed: the children were each given a part of the serum, and all of them scattered, bitterly divided. Olivia had not been able to hold her family together. The serum had been too powerful. Just as for generations of Cahills, as Olivia had foreseen. Murder, plots, lies, revenge . . . stretching out for five centuries, pitting Cahill against Cahill.

Misery handed down, generation after generation.

Yet beneath my beating Heart my Secret gave me joy and hope.

That was Madeleine, the child Olivia was carrying when she fled the destruction of her home.

Then references to gathering . . . what? To make a dram—a bit of the serum?

No, Amy thought. *Olivia hates the serum. That is clear.*

My Joy, my Song, you have my charge.

She's telling Madeleine to do something. . . .

Amy sat up in bed. Could it be? It made sense. It made *perfect* sense.

"Yes!" she cried. This was it, this was the answer. This was the key!

She ran across the hall to Dan's room. She shook him awake.

He bolted up. "What's happening? Where's my pants?"

"Dan, wake up! I've been reading Olivia's book." Amy waited until the sleepy confusion left Dan's eyes. "I think I know what Olivia was working on. She was formulating the *antidote* for the serum. That's the key to stopping Pierce!"

CHAPTER 16

Attleboro, Massachusetts

The house felt so big without Fiske and Amy and Dan. Nellie wasn't used to such silence. It seemed to echo against her ears. When she walked across the polished wood floor, her footsteps had sounded as loud as a giant's. She'd kicked off her boots and was now padding around in her socks.

Anxiety gnawed at her. She'd run into a big, fat dead end. It was like Sammy had disappeared into thin air.

She reached into her pocket and brought out the New Jersey Turnpike ticket. Whoever had used it had traveled the entire distance — the turnpike ended at the Delaware Memorial Bridge.

She recognized Pony's knock — three rhythmic taps. Then the taps turned into pounding. She ran to let him in, her phone still in her hand. Pony stepped inside, took one look at her open laptop, and crossed to it in two steps.

"What are you doing?" Nellie asked as he quickly began typing.

"Catching a mouse," he said.

"I thought you said that laptop was safe."

"It was." Pony kept typing, his clumsy hands agile on the keys. "I got you, mousie," he murmured. "Follow the cheese. . . ."

"Are you writing to someone?"

"Code. I'm hunting them while they're hunting me."

"But you'll lead them here!"

"You swine!" Pony slapped his hand down on the table, then resumed typing. "Not you, goddess. Listen, it's not . . . here . . . I'm worried about. They *know* where you are. It's . . . Dan and Amy . . ."

"They're tracking *them*?"

"They're trying. Did you receive an attachment from them?"

"Just a photograph . . ."

Pony muttered through his teeth. "I'm rerouting . . . through Johannesburg . . . to Beijing. . . . And then . . . come on, mousie, follow me. . . . "

Nellie crossed her fingers, then closed her eyes.

"GOTCHA!" Pony closed the laptop with a smash.

"Did it work?" Nellie asked.

"They are probably right now looking in Mozambique."

"Could you track their computer?"

Pony shook his head. "Almost got them, but I can't pinpoint it. It's not in the US. Somewhere in Europe."

"That doesn't exactly narrow it down."

He scratched his ear. "Best I could do in thirty seconds. But I can't be one hundred percent sure they didn't get a general location on D and A before I managed to divert them."

"I'd better tell Dan and Amy to get out of there."

"Not with that phone, you're not." Pony held out his hand. "Did you connect the phone to the laptop at any time?"

"The photo came in as a text so I downloaded the photo. . . ."

He dropped the phone on the floor and smashed it with his shoe. "Annoyed!"

"Pony, you're scaring me."

He faced her, his hands deep in his pockets. "You should be scared. We should all be scared. This situation is completely wreckitudinous. We have been chomped by the supreme empress."

"Pony, I'm begging you now. Please speak English. It is our common language." Nellie tucked her hands in her armpits. She hated it when her hands started to shake. By the look on Pony's face, she knew it was bad.

Whatever Pony would tell her, she knew one thing: It was time to overrule Amy. They needed help.

He sighed as he sifted the phone through his fingers and dropped it in his pocket. "I figured out who hacked into your system. Who is probably *still* trying to track you."

"Who?" Nellie asked, bewildered. Whoever it was, there was a look of fear on Pony's face.

He leaned in and lowered his voice, as though the house itself was no longer safe. Maybe it wasn't.

"Waldo," he whispered.

CHAPTER 17

An undisclosed location

April May got her first cell phone at four. Of course it was an old one of her mother's and she couldn't make a call on it, but it was her favorite toy. She took it apart, which made her parents laugh. But when, at ten, she opened up her father's motherboard, they didn't take it so well.

April had always had a thing for secrets. When other children had imaginary best friends, she constructed her own multiple identities. She could be anyone she liked on the Internet. That was freedom, something in short supply in her house. Her mother wanted to know everything she was thinking and her father wanted to know everything she was doing.

There was no privacy in her household. The one time she tried to keep a diary, her father read it, then returned it with his own corrections in red pen. Her mother copied it and sent it to her own therapist so she could discuss April's problems "in the context of my own personhood."

April soon learned to fabricate a false front, a place where her parents could access her, while her real self roamed free somewhere else: in her imagination, her dreams . . . and the Internet. That was when she first realized that there, people could be anything they wanted. They could visit sites, write e-mails, join communities that had nothing to do with their real selves.

She never cared for school-yard games. She'd rather sneak back into the classroom and hack into her teacher's cell phone, then read all the e-mails. Secrets were power.

Her parents soon learned to change their passwords often. It didn't help much. She still hacked into her father's e-mail when she was twelve. She didn't like what she found there, but she used it. The next thing she knew, she was in boarding school. That's when her hacking really began.

At school, as her skills increased, she discovered that there was a whole shadow world out there, filled with people just like her. People who saw that digital firewalls were just a challenge to be overcome. April worked less and less on social studies and field hockey and music and math, all those high school preoccupations that suddenly seemed lame compared to this thrilling, secret world. Why bother studying for a math test when you could tell your teacher that you know about his secret weekend trips to that casino in

Atlantic City—the trips his wife doesn't know about? Why bother befriending a roommate who you know is sending texts about how weird you are? Easier to live in a shadow world.

But even April had scruples. Exposing hypocrisy was her game. She didn't hack to destroy, only to reveal. Sure, she could hack into the CIA, but did she want to? Not yet, anyway.

In the past year or two, she had found another thrill: making money. Lots of it. For certain select clients, money was no object. She was choosy about her clients. She'd only hack into the accounts of people or organizations she didn't approve of. Actors, politicians, silly celebrities, billionaires who got that way by lying, cheating, and stealing.

She named her company WALDO. She employed a few good hackers, but only a few. No one had ever seen her. There were no photographs of April May on the Internet, and she intended to keep it that way.

She now had a comfortable couple of million dollars or so residing in a very secure account in the Cayman Islands.

Her latest client, J. Rutherford Pierce, was possibly her biggest yet. She didn't like him much, but he tested her abilities, and that was a good thing. Thanks to him, she'd broken into several search engines and manipulated results. He had his eye on a political career, and April May had discovered early on in this business that almost everyone had something to hide.

He was going places, too. Through him, she could break into media and possibly politics, and then the sky was the limit.

And she didn't like two rich entitled brats with everything in the world they needed causing trouble wherever they went, either. So. If trading information for cash meant you humiliated people in a handful of tabloids, maybe seriously mess with their lives . . . hey, it was a living.

They'd hired some expert security control, that was for sure. Walls behind walls. April was almost beginning to enjoy the game.

The kids weren't in Mozambique. That she knew for sure. The hacker could send a false chain, but she wasn't about to pick it up.

She tapped in another line of code. April leaned forward. This was good news she could pass along to her latest client. The Cahill account was heating up.

CHAPTER 18

Somewhere over the west of Ireland

Below them, stone walls, green fields, patches of yellow, patches of rust. White puffy clouds in a blue sky. It was a fine day to fly. Pierce's hands rested lightly on the controls. He loved small planes. He didn't like highways. He was always in a hurry now that he had someplace to get to. He looked down at his hands. One day soon they'd hold all the power in the world.

Very soon.

Every step he'd planned so meticulously had worked.

Media mogul. *Check.*

Millions of followers. *Check.*

Financing from secretive billionaires. *Check.*

Secret army. *On track.*

Stockpile of weaponry. *Check.*

Next: the United States presidency.

And now, the final push. Announce his candidacy. Hire Atlas to start some sort of war somewhere.

Detonate a couple of warheads. Then blame the current US president for it.

Galt and Cara sat in the seats behind him. They looked bored. They wouldn't be soon enough.

Such perfect politician's children—he'd made sure of that. Sporty boy, musical girl. Blond and even-featured like their mother. Cara was pretty—a bit on the bland side, like Debi Ann—but that worked in his favor. Politicians with gorgeous daughters got the wrong kind of media attention. The focus needed to be on *him*. Handsome Galt, only thirteen and already looking like Pierce. Straight nose, good chin, gray eyes. Killer instinct.

Thanks to his new regime for the kids, they had shed doubt, defiance, pounds, ethics . . . all those pesky things he used to despise in them.

"Hey, kids," he called over the noise of the engine. "How are you feeling since I started you on those smoothies? Stronger, am I right? Maybe even smarter? Quicker?"

"I feel awesome," Galt said.

"Super, Dad," Cara said. Why did she always sound like she was mocking him? Pierce glanced at her quickly, but she stared peacefully back.

"What are you thinking right now?" he fired at her.

"I enjoy the mango flavor best," she answered promptly.

"Not a very interesting thought," Pierce said. "But acceptable."

It started as a game when they were young. How they used to squeal with pleasure when he asked them the question! He had invented the game. They had to answer within one second, so that he could be sure they weren't lying. Little did they know, at three, at four, at five, that he was training them. What was the use of having children unless you could count on their loyalty?

Every morning he rose early enough to scan the newspapers. He cut out the articles he wanted them to read and placed them by their plates. Evenings were for printouts and magazine articles. He was forming their minds so that they would be just like him.

Lately he'd been thinking that the web was too vast to control. He was drawing up a plan to delete certain parts of history from it, so that his kids couldn't access stories unless he approved.

Cara was reaching for her earphones. He'd lose her to a symphony in a second. He needed her attention.

"Kids, remember, it's our secret, right? Your mom—you know how she is. She'd want to protect her babies. She'd still have you on applesauce and mashed carrots if she could."

Galt snickered.

"Are you ready for one last test? Are you up for it?"

"Yeah!" Galt said, pumping a fist. "Bring it on!"

"I know you're loyal," Pierce said. "I know you're smart. I know you are in excellent physical condition.

What I don't know—and I need to—is that you can operate independently."

Cara looked warily at him. "What do you mean?"

"I need to know that you can be dropped into a situation—*any* situation—navigate through it, and deliver results. Are you ready for your assignment?"

"Ready," Galt said.

"I've got reporters all over the globe looking for Amy and Dan Cahill. Those two drive web traffic like nobody's business. I have a location where they *were*, but I don't know where they *are*."

"Are we heading to London?" Cara asked.

"Not yet. We're over the west coast of Ireland now. Your assignment is to find Amy and Dan Cahill and pass along their coordinates to me in time for me to send some paparazzi their way."

The two kids looked dubious. Pierce needed them to buy into this. He could hardly send his bodyguards swarming over the Irish countryside. Galt and Cara would be perfect. Nobody paid attention to kids.

"Just pretend you're students backpacking around Europe," he told them.

"This doesn't sound very challenging," Galt said sulkily.

"I think it sounds fun," Cara said, peering out the window. "It's a beautiful country. And as long as I don't have to sleep outdoors, I'm cool with it."

That's good, because you don't have a choice, Pierce thought, but he knew better than to say it.

"Where are the backpacks?" Cara asked.

"Right behind your seats. With the parachutes. Tony will help you into the gear."

The man the kids had assumed was a steward came forward from where he'd been sitting in the back, well out of earshot.

"P-parachutes?" Cara sputtered. "But we've never skydived!"

"Not to worry. Didn't I say you were in top physical condition?"

Tony began to slide a chute over Galt's shoulders.

"Dad? I'm not so sure about this!" Galt exclaimed. "Couldn't you find a nice airport to land in?"

"Don't want to leave a paper trail," Pierce said. "Besides, this will be fun. I'm looking out for you guys."

"I don't want to d-do this," Cara said as Tony steered her toward the back of the plane.

"Stop whining," Pierce said, and Tony opened the cabin door.

When Amy and Dan cycled into the village the next morning, Fiona poked her head out of the grocery and gestured at them frantically. They hurried inside, and she closed and locked the door.

"I've got a message for you from home," she said. "Your phones are no longer safe. You're supposed to destroy them. If you need to communicate, you're to go to an Internet café. There's one in the next village. And there is a very slight chance your location was compromised. The advice is to stay put for now. I'm supposed to tell you that a pony is checking everything out?"

"Okay," Amy said, nodding. She felt her nerves strain at the news.

"Don't worry. We'll keep you safe. The whole village is on alert. Which is why . . ." Fiona crossed to the window and peered out behind the shade. Then she let it drop. "There's someone in town asking for directions to Bhaile Anois," she said. "He checked in late last night at the inn."

Amy and Dan exchanged uneasy glances.

"What does he look like?" Amy asked.

Fiona narrowed her eyes. "Sneaky, for certain," she said. "And he's quite a waster. Good for nothin' but complaining. Nora over at the inn said he's never satisfied with the temperature of his tea, and he asked for a cashmere throw in his room."

Amy and Dan exchanged another glance.

"IAN," they said together, and sighed.

"You *know* the eejit?" Fiona asked.

"The eejit is our cousin," Amy said.

"*Distant* cousin," Dan added. "Very, very distant."

They strolled over to the front of the inn, where Ian Kabra stood outside arguing with the desk clerk. Their tall, elegant cousin propped a rickety bicycle up with one index finger, as if it would contaminate him. In this rural village, he was dressed in pressed jeans, a navy jacket, and a silky dark T-shirt. He was only sixteen, but he looked older.

"Are you seriously telling me, my good man, that this is the only transportation in the village? Surely there is a car service. Or a garage, where one might hire a car? Even in this backwater?"

The red-haired young man put his hands on his hips. "Why don't you do this, me boyo? Take a flying leap at the nearest garage yourself? And then you can—"

Dan strode forward and took Ian's arm. "We'll take it from here. Thanks."

"Dan! Amy! Thank goodness you're here," Ian said in his plummy British accent. "The locals have been *supremely* unhelpful."

"Ian—"

He narrowed his dark eyes. "I was lost on the back roads for hours last night because when I asked some villager if this was Meenalappa, she said no. And I was standing *right in the middle of the village*! If I ever see that young woman again, I'll—" Ian's eyes widened. Fiona was crossing the street to the pub. "Th-there she is!" he sputtered.

"Hi, Fiona!" Dan said, waving.

"Hi, Danny boy!" she trilled back.

"You're *acquainted* with that creature?"

"Relax, Ian." Dan tried to hide his grin. "She was just trying to protect us."

"Did Nellie call you?" Amy asked, irritation spiking her question.

"Of course she did. And Hamilton and Jonah, too," Ian said, naming their other cousins. "They're on alert. Reagan and Madison would come, too, but they're both training for the Olympics, and Hamilton wouldn't let them. They're on reserve, though."

Amy gritted her teeth. "I told Nellie not to alert anyone."

"Nonsense," Ian said briskly. "We're Cahills. We're in this together. Now, let's go to Grace's house. It's got to be better than that shoddy inn."

Ian sniffed at the single bed with the cotton coverlet and plain white sheets. "I spoke too soon. Why, oh why, didn't Grace know about thread counts?" he moaned.

"I have no idea what you mean, dude, but if you insult Grace in my presence again you are going to have one very fat lip," Dan replied cheerfully. "Or two."

"I'm not insulting her," Ian said. "I'm just indicating my preference. If only Natalie were here, she would know exactly what I mean."

Suddenly, Ian's face clouded. Natalie had died only six months ago and she'd been his baby sister. Amy knew the wound must still be so unbearably fresh.

Ian cleared his throat and quickly turned away. His voice came out higher and constricted. "Since I'm alone in this, I won't say another word. I will cope with threadbare towels and scratchy sheets like a gentleman."

Amy could tell by the way Ian was examining his bedding that he was close to tears. Nobody was *that* interested in fluffing their pillow.

"We miss her, too, Ian," she said gently.

He cleared his throat. "Thanks."

It would be like losing Dan, she thought. She had a glimpse into great and unquenchable grief, and if she could have produced a cashmere throw for Ian at that moment, she would have been happy to provide it.

"We really need your help," she added.

Ian's face brightened, and she knew it had been the right thing to say. He wanted to be needed now.

Ian followed them down the stairs. "I know you two are going to need some Lucian strategy." He lowered himself onto the overstuffed sofa. "So relax and tell me how I can solve all your problems."

It was almost a flashback to the former arrogant Ian they'd known, but now he ended the remark with a smile that mocked his old self-centeredness. The loss of Natalie had changed him.

Amy felt her eyes mist. With all her worrying about putting him in danger, she hadn't stopped to consider that Ian might need them, too.

They sat outside on the back lawn. Amy had spread out a linen blanket and brought a tray with a teapot and pretty mismatched cups — Grace had always collected mismatched china — and a plate of cookies. The weather had warmed and brightened, and the soft breeze ruffled the pages of Olivia's book.

Ian knew more Latin than Amy, so he was able to translate a few things that had stumped her.

"This dowry reference is puzzling," Ian said. "She

keeps referring to it, but we don't know what it is. Is it land, or money, or animals, or objects?"

"It does come up often," Amy agreed. "Even after Gideon is dead."

Amy looked up at him. Their faces were very close. She remembered when those dark expressive eyes would make her quiver inside, when being this close would make her blush and stammer. Not anymore, though.

A shadow fell over the blanket.

"Well, well. Aren't you two cozy."

Shading her eyes, Amy looked up and, with a spurt of uncomfortable surprise, saw Jake. Her heart began to pound. He was standing against the sun, and she couldn't see his expression.

It was official. She was going to kill Nellie.

Guiltily, she scrambled to her feet. Now she could see his face, his strong nose, brown eyes, dark messy hair. He looked tired. And angry. "What are you doing here?" she asked, flustered.

"Nellie contacted us and said you needed help."

"I told her not to do that!"

"Yes, I can see why." Jake's gaze flicked to Ian. "You already reached out for help, didn't you? Sorry to interrupt the tea party."

"Our network went down," she said. "We even had to give up our phones. I couldn't text you."

He gave a tense shrug. "Doesn't matter. You don't

have to hit me over the head. I get it." His stony gaze moved to Ian.

"No, you *don't* get it," Amy said.

Ian rose. "Good to see you, Jake," he said. "I hope you brought your little brother. There's some medieval Italian to translate. . . ."

Just then Atticus bounded up with Dan. Atticus was Jake's half brother, but they didn't look much alike. Atticus was wiry and intense, and he'd inherited his African-American's mother's thick curly hair, which he wore in shoulder-length dreadlocks.

"Isn't this fantastic?" Dan asked. "Jake and Atticus in person!" Dan punched Atticus on the arm. "Professor! You are *so* busted for showing up without telling!"

"You don't have a phone!" Atticus said with a grin. "It was an insurmountable impediment, dude!"

Although Atticus was a year and a half younger than Dan, he made up for it with a vocabulary that could make a college professor hit the dictionary.

"Aren't you supposed to be in college?" Dan asked. "How'd you get time off?"

"Taking independent study," Atticus explained. "Dad said I should put off Harvard until I was emotionally mature enough to go."

"Emotionally mature?" Dan hooted. "Your pop will have to wait about a billion years, dude!"

"I won't have to wait as long as you, dude!" Atticus adjusted his glasses as he peered down at the blanket. "Hey, is that the book Nellie told us about?"

Jake's eyes flicked to Olivia's book. "You've got it outside in the *sun*? Are you out of your minds?"

Amy crossed her arms. "We're being careful."

"It's not about careful, this is a five-hundred-year-old manuscript! You should be wearing gloves—Atticus brought some—and keeping it *out* of the sunlight."

"It didn't take you long to start barking orders!" Amy exclaimed, her face flushing. "But then you always know best, don't you?"

"Somebody has to be mature in this situation," Jake said, his gaze flashing at Ian, who was now intently trying to brush cookie crumbs off his pants.

"True. In that case, we'd rather consult your little brother," Ian said with a smirk. "Medieval manuscripts are his field, am I right?"

"Technically, it's early Renaissance," Jake said.

"Thanks for the correction, my good man. Amy is right—you *do* know best." Ian slipped his arm around Amy. "She's so perceptive. One of the many things I adore about her."

"It's getting chilly. Why don't we go inside?" Amy suggested brightly as she tried to step out of the circle of Ian's arm.

Ian took the opportunity to rub her shoulder. "You do feel rather cold," he said. "Let's sit by the fire. Jake, since you're so interested in proper handling, why don't you take the book?"

Jake snatched up the book and furiously stomped off toward the house.

"You forgot to wear gloves!" Ian called after him.

Amy pushed him away. "Really, Ian."

"What a touchy guy," Ian said. "Frankly, I don't know what you see in him."

He winced as the kitchen door slammed, then glanced at Amy's red face. "Hmmm. It might be a good time for me to take a walk," Ian said.

CHAPTER 20

The house was suddenly too crowded.

Within a couple of hours, it had been transformed. The lively, focused curiosity of the Rosenbloom brothers made the air buzz. The living room was now strewn with teacups and wadded-up napkins and plates with half-eaten sandwiches, and shoes on the floor and pencils snapped in half and discarded scratch paper and Atticus's toothbrush, because Atticus said he got his best ideas while he was brushing his teeth.

Jake's laptop was secure, so at least they could now do research on the web. Through their father, Dr. Mark Rosenbloom, an archaeologist, they had access to online libraries that Amy and Dan could never have consulted. Since spending the winter in Rome, Jake's Italian was close to fluent, and Atticus was a Latin scholar. They had translated in a few hours what would have taken her days.

"My question is this: Why was an Irish woman back then fluent in Italian?" Jake asked. "Highly unusual."

"She was a scholar," Amy said. "She mentions that her father taught her Latin."

"Latin I understand, even though it's unusual for her to learn it," Jake said.

"She did come from a family of bards, Jake," Atticus said.

"Beards?" Dan asked.

"Bards," Atticus said with a snort of laughter. "Poets. The learned scholars of Ireland."

"I bet they had beards, though," Dan said, and Atticus laughed and threw an eraser at him.

"The Irish have an amazing scholarly history," Jake said. "Bards were more than poets. They founded schools, usually had nobleman patrons. They were revered in Ireland. But—"

"They were all men," Amy finished. "Typical."

"It just doesn't add up," Jake said, frowning. "And this code in the back . . ."

"Is that unusual, too?" Dan asked.

"Yes and no," Jake said. "Actually, cryptography was widely used in sixteenth-century Europe. Queen Elizabeth had a school for espionage. It was a little later, but still, I'm not surprised at the code. But why is she using it in a household accounts book? And it's so odd looking . . . reminds me of something I can't place."

"You know what Dad says," Atticus put in. "When you're stumped, return to the source." He turned to Amy. "Can I look at the secret room?"

"Sure. I'll show you."

They took the stairs up to the second floor. Amy pulled down the sconce, and the stairs rose.

"That is just amazing-cool," Atticus said, bounding into the space. He peered at her, his eyes wide and curious behind his glasses. "Do you think Grace could have left you a clue? About the code in the book, I mean. Dan told me she left a clue about the alphabet lock."

"If she did, I don't know what it is." Amy plopped tiredly in the white chair, her hands clasped. "She said the struggle never ends. That it's only abandoned. She *knew* that even if we destroyed the serum we could never be free."

"That's what spooks Dan," Atticus said, prowling around the room. "He keeps waiting to have a regular life. It never happens. He's super scared it never will."

She smiled weakly. "How come you know my brother better than I do?"

"Aw. With Dan you have to listen to his underneath, you know? Not so much what he says. Anyway, I know how he feels. Ever since my mom died, my dad thinks he's Indiana Jones. I keep waiting for him to settle down, but instead Jake and I just get yanked around the world."

"I'm sorry, Atticus," Amy said. "I thought you liked living in Rome."

He smiled. "I do. *Now.* I just had to let go of wanting something else, that's all. And realize my life is pretty cool. And having a brother like Jake raise me is amazing-cool, too."

"I always knew you were smart," Amy said. "But I didn't know you were so wise."

"Not so smart if I can't help you," Atticus said, blushing furiously. "So is there anything else here that would give you a hint? Is there anything odd, anything in the room that just doesn't seem like Grace?"

"It's all Grace, really," Amy said. "She loved white and blue. The table is old, the Windsor chair . . ." She looked across the room and saw herself reflected in the mirror, a girl without a clue. "Everything but that mirror, I guess. I mean, she didn't like ornate things, and it's gold . . . and if you sit in this chair, you look right at yourself. . . ."

Atticus looked at the mirror. He pushed his glasses up his nose in the characteristic gesture that meant he was thinking hard. Then he spun around and laughed. "My brain is exploding! Amy — it's the easiest code in the *world*! It's not just code, it's mirror writing!"

"Mirror writing? Are you sure?"

"Elementary! Come on!"

They hurried downstairs, where Atticus excitedly told the others about his discovery.

"Of course!" Jake exclaimed. He hit himself lightly on the side of the head. "Sometimes things are *too* obvious."

"This shouldn't be so hard," Atticus said. "Olivia is writing an instruction to Madeleine, right? 'My Joy, my Song, you have my charge.' If she made it too hard, Madeleine wouldn't have been able to figure it out."

"That's why the references might have been things that they both knew," Jake said, tapping his pencil against the desk. "A family vocab. Like the way Grace spoke to Amy and Dan. Using the familiar."

"Maybe it has something to do with the teacher Olivia talks about in the poem?" Amy asked. *"'Mio maestro.'"*

"It's more than a teacher, actually," Jake said. *"'. . . mio maestro di vita.'* Teacher of life. It implies someone who teaches more than facts—all the aspects of life, a way to live. . . . Like a mentor."

Dan recited from memory. "'. . . and take up battle not with arms but wisdom gained from ancient land / kept close and passed from hand to hand / to *mio maestro di vita*, thee of timeless woman, universal man.'"

Atticus sat up, his dreads flying. "What did Grace say in her letter?" he asked Amy with sudden urgency. "About the struggle?"

Amy picked up Grace's journal. "'I am sorry to say that our struggle is never finished, only abandoned.'" She looked up. The two brothers were rising from their chairs, their faces full of disbelief, discovery, revelation. . . .

She rose to her feet. "What?"

"'Art is never finished, only abandoned'!" Atticus crowed. "It's a quote. Quite famous, actually."

"Not to us, dude," Dan said.

"There's an old game Jake and I used to play. You know how you memorize quotes from famous people in history?"

"Constantly," Dan said.

"And the mirror," Jake said. "And universal man, of course! *Vitruvian Man!*"

Amy frowned. "That famous drawing of the man with his arms out? But that's by . . ."

"And timeless woman!" Atticus crowed. "The *Mona Lisa!*"

Amy felt the knowledge roar through her body. "Are you talking about *Leonardo da Vinci?*"

"Gosh," Dan said. "Even I've heard of him."

"Leonardo was Olivia's teacher," Atticus said. "*That's* why she knew Italian."

Jake excitedly returned to the book. "That's what the coded pages are. An account of her travels, but in it there must be something Leonardo gave her. 'Then he to me bequeathed it, and with instruction bid / and I, through his own methods, hid.' Now that we know this, we can crack the code, I know we can."

"This is so amazing," Atticus breathed. He stared at Dan and Amy in wonder, as though they were suddenly priceless works of art. "The most famous man in the Renaissance, and he *taught* your great-great . . ."

". . . great-great et cetera grandmother," Dan finished.

"The antidote is in those coded pages," Amy said. "I just know it."

Which makes the book just as dangerous as the serum. Because if we possess it, someone else will want it.

Yes, Grace. The struggle never ends. You knew that.

Jake sat, writing notes on a piece of scrap paper. Atticus tapped his toothbrush on the table as he looked over Jake's shoulder. He was kicking his long, skinny legs, and his feet in bright red socks looked too big for his body.

He was just a kid.

And Jake . . . the way he made room for Atticus, the way he casually put his hand on the tapping toothbrush to stop it . . .

Jake was Atticus's caretaker, his protector. They had a distant dad, a dead mother. The two of them would be lost without each other.

Here they were, alive in the moment, precious life coursing through them.

If she allowed them to help, they could die.

And she would be standing over another open grave.

So much emotion welled up in her chest that she was afraid she'd burst into sobs.

Amy cleared her throat. She looked at the two brothers.

"You're going to have to leave," she said.

CHAPTER 21

Ian had jumped on a bike and headed in the opposite direction from Meenalappa. It had taken him exactly three minutes to realize the place was a backwater. A pub, a grocery, a church, and a store selling rubber boots and tweed caps. No, thank you. He would head to the larger village of Ballycreel.

He pedaled hard, cooling his hot cheeks. For once he didn't mind the mist. If it wasn't raining in Ireland, it was about to or just did.

He probably should have been nicer to Jake. It wasn't that he didn't like the guy. It was just that when Jake and Atticus had showed up, he'd gotten, well . . .

Jealous.

Jealous of the way Amy suddenly had eyes for nobody but Jake and was trying so hard to hide it. How Dan lit up when he saw Atticus.

Nobody lit up for Ian.

He knew he wasn't the *nicest* person. . . .

Natalie understood him. She had been equally as . . . not nice as he was.

But he was trying! He was learning! People didn't get nice by accident, did they? They had parents who were nice. Nice to their kids, nice to others. His parents . . . well, they didn't understand the concept of "nice."

And they never, ever would have understood the concept of "lonely."

That word had never been in the Kabra vocab, but it had been bouncing around Ian's head lately. It was shocking how many times he found himself saying, *"If only Natalie were here . . ."*

He had fought with Natalie and been bored by Natalie and sometimes even felt he despised her, but she'd been his best friend. Maybe his only friend.

Losing his sister . . . well, it had turned out to be much harder than he expected. Sure, he no longer had to follow Natalie around Harrods, holding her purchases, but he didn't know what he was supposed to *do*, exactly. When Nellie had called to say that Amy and Dan needed his help, he had sprung into action immediately. He'd packed a few things and taken off. He hadn't even pressed his trousers.

Nobody likes you, nobody likes you, nobody likes you.
My sister is dead, my sister is dead. . . .

The bicycle wheels went round and round, slithering on the wet country road. The words in his head revolved.

And suddenly he realized he was far from the cottage, and lost.

The mist was now rain. Ian wanted to kick himself, but he'd probably fall off the bike.

He bumped off to the side to turn the bike around and took out his phone to consult GPS. Then he remembered that Pony had disabled it for safety reasons. The protective cover told him to KEEP CALM AND CARRY ON. He snorted at that. Did he really have a choice right now?

At that moment, a Range Rover barreled around the curve, sending him diving into the grass. The car smashed into his bike, which flew after him.

The Range Rover driver slammed on the brakes. With a squeal of tires, it backed up.

"You bloody fool!" Ian shouted.

A girl with red hair stuck her head out of the driver's side window. "Well, *that* didn't go well. What were you doing in the middle of the road?" she asked. He heard the lilt of a brogue in her voice. He couldn't wait to get back to London, where people didn't have *music* in their voices.

Ian popped to his feet. "I was not in the middle of the road! I was on the shoulder!"

"In case you haven't noticed, this road doesn't have a shoulder," she answered. "It's a country lane, not much wider than a path, actually. You have to watch yourself on our roads, you tourists."

Ian bristled at being called a tourist. "Maybe you have to watch your driving!"

She smiled, and Ian suddenly noticed that the girl was ravishingly pretty. She had one dimple in her left cheek. What kind of a girl had only one dimple? Ian didn't care for asymmetry, but somehow this particular one . . . worked.

"Sure, I suppose I do," she said. "But it's my da's car, and so I like to give it a workout and bring it back muddy. By the way, are you all right?"

"Think so, thanks for the afterthought," Ian said.

Her smile turned into a grin. She opened the door and jumped out. "Oh, dear, look at your bicycle. I'm afraid it's rather smashed."

Ian saw that the front wheel had bent. "This just tops off my day."

"Don't fret, I've got a nice big car and time on my hands."

Before Ian could protest, she had lifted up the bike with surprising ease and deposited it in the trunk of the car. "Now. Where can I drop you?"

Normally, this would count as one stellar day. He'd gladly trade a smashed bicycle for a pretty girl in a very expensive car. But not today. He had to get back to Bhaile Anois. The argument with Jake had been petty and stupid.

"Don't worry, I'm not a criminal. I'm just a girl in her daddy's car who is willing to rescue you. I'm Maura, by the way."

"Roger," Ian said, because while this was an extremely pretty girl, he was still a Lucian, and a Kabra. Any personal information was on a need-to-know basis.

"Hey now, you dropped your phone." She bent and picked it up and handed it to him. Their fingers touched, briefly, and Ian felt something, some kind of charge from just touching her skin.

He felt his face heat up. That *never* happened. To cover, he dropped the phone in his pocket. "You could give me a lift to Ballycreel." The village was big enough that it would provide cover. And he could hike back to Bhaile Anois from there.

"Are you staying there, then? At the Arms, or the Pocket of Fish?"

"Pocket of Fish," Ian said.

"Climb in," she said. "I know a shortcut."

Ian climbed in. Maura took off, driving way too fast. Ian tried not to clutch the door handle.

"We live in Dublin, but we have a house down in Doolin. A castle, more like. I prefer an Irish castle to a Scottish one, don't you? A better sense of scale. The more modern, the better, if you ask me. Those sixteenth-century ones are drafty, no matter how much they pump up the central heating."

Okay, not only was she pretty but she could compare the merits of *castles*. This was his type of girl.

"I don't have that much experience with castles," Ian said. Despite the fact that his father now lived in one.

She gave him a quick once-over. "Don't be so modest. Your jacket is cashmere from Brioni's last season. Your shoes are handmade from John Lobb. And don't get me started on your haircut."

"Actually, I prefer an estate," Ian said. "Early nineteenth century, with central heating. You're right. Castles are drafty."

She grinned. "Here's the shortcut."

She jerked the wheel, and the Range Rover slammed onto a dirt track that was probably for sheep. Over the rattle of the car, Ian shouted, "Is this a *road*?"

"It is if I say it is!" Maura shouted. "I told you I liked to bring it back muddy! I only like my da when he's fuming!"

She gave a peal of laughter that made Ian join in. He'd heard the term *infectious laughter* before, but he never quite understood it. He rarely laughed, and certainly wouldn't do it just because someone else did.

But as the Range Rover hit a ditch and his head bumped the ceiling, he didn't care. He just kept on laughing.

She dropped him on the main street of Ballycreel. Ian hauled the bicycle out of the trunk.

"I'd offer to pay for it, but I know you can afford it," she said.

A small spot of mud was on Maura's (undimpled) cheek. Her face was flushed from their wild ride, and her green eyes danced.

It made his heart leap, somehow. Odd feeling.

"Thanks for the ride," he said. "If you can call it that."

"Call me sometime," she said. She tucked a small card into his pocket.

With one last flirtatious look, she hopped back into the car and took off.

Ian stared down at the card. MAURA DEVON CARLISLE. There was a number below it. The card stock was smooth and heavy in his hand. The typeface discreet, yet bold. Exactly what he would have chosen.

As soon as the Range Rover was out of sight, he tore up the card and threw it away.

Better not to be tempted. Better to let it go.

Ian left the bicycle in an alley. He started the long walk back to Bhaile Anois, his footsteps on the asphalt road, his pace steady and sure in his expensive hand-made shoes.

Lonely. Lonely. Lonely.

CHAPTER 22

Atticus stopped swinging his legs. Jake sat staring at Amy. Dan sat up on the couch. His sister's green eyes were usually warm, but now they looked as hard as metal. What was she doing?

"What did you say?" Atticus asked.

Amy lifted her chin. "This is a Cahill matter. It's our problem to solve."

"Excuse me?" Jake asked. "Atticus just broke the mirror code. Do you realize what you have here in this book? It is an immeasurable gift to scholarship — who knows what it contains about Leonardo!"

"This isn't a college *seminar*," Amy said evenly. "This is a *battle*. And it's not yours. We are grateful for your help. But you should head back to Rome first thing in the morning."

"But —" Dan started, but Amy silenced him with her *stay out of this* look. Dan snapped his mouth shut, but he felt his blood beginning to boil.

Jake's mouth hung open. He looked as though

he'd just been punched in the head. Or the stomach. Someplace really, really bad.

"This is about family," Amy said. "The Cahills can take it from here."

Atticus looked as though he was about to cry. Behind his glasses, he was blinking rapidly.

"Hey," Dan said, "can we take a vote on this?"

"No." Amy's voice was firm. "I'm the head of the family. This is my call."

"You may be the head," Dan said furiously. "You're not a *dictator*!"

Ian walked through the door. "You're not going to believe what happened to me—" he started, then stopped, his gaze moving from Jake to Amy to Dan to Atticus. He tossed his phone on the desk. "What did I miss?"

His phone landed right next to Jake's. Dan read the words. KEEP CALM AND CARRY ON. How odd that the two boys, so different in temperament, had the same phone case. The well-known phrase bounced around his head. He didn't feel calm. He didn't feel like carrying on. He wanted to throw both phones into the toilet for telling him to do such a lame thing when all he wanted to do was yell and change what was happening.

"Nothing," Jake said. "You didn't miss a thing."

"She didn't mean it," Atticus whispered to Jake later. "I could tell by her eyes."

Jake was balling up clothes and shoving them into his pack. "She meant every word."

"Jake, if you could just talk to her—"

"I've talked to her. Listen, little bro, we're done here. This is the last piece of business we'll do for the *Cahills*." He said the last word bitterly.

"She doesn't really want us to go," Atticus said miserably. "And Dan definitely doesn't!"

"Dan is not the boss. Amy is. As she made very clear." Jake zipped up his pack. "Get your stuff together. I called the village and hired a car. We're leaving first thing in the morning for the airport."

First light. Amy heard the faint thud of the door closing. She ran to the window. The dark shapes of Jake and Atticus headed toward a car in the drive. Atticus seemed crushed by the enormous backpack he wore on his shoulders. Jake had slung his pack over one shoulder, and he strode quickly toward the car, as if he couldn't get away fast enough.

She wanted to run downstairs, throw open the door, and beg them to stop. Instead, she looked away.

Her door creaked open. Dan stuck his head in. "You're awake." He hovered in the doorway. "That was a really lousy thing to do."

Amy pressed her forehead against the cold glass. "Dan, do you remember being on that bridge? Do you remember that terror? How can I ask them to risk their lives for us?"

"You're not *asking* anything of anybody," Dan said. "We're all volunteers here. And I know one thing. You're wrong. Jake and Atticus *are* family. You're turning into Aunt Beatrice!"

"That's not fair!" Amy cried. "I *have* to make the decisions. You're the one who wants to leave the family! Why should *you* get a vote, Dan? You opted out, remember?"

"I'm here right now!" Dan shot back. "Watching you be mean!"

They stared at each other, furious.

They heard an insistent pounding downstairs. She and Dan dove for the stairs.

Amy got to the door first. Fiona's hand was raised to knock again, her dark hair shimmering with droplets from the dawn mist. "There's a black SUV in the village," she said. "They're looking for you. You've got to clear out."

Amy's head cleared and she snapped into survival mode. "How?"

"Boat."

"Give us five minutes."

Amy and Dan raced upstairs and woke Ian. They threw things into backpacks, wrapped Olivia's book in a waterproof bag, and within five minutes had locked up the house and run down to the dock.

Fiona stood on the deck of a small motorboat. She

reached out a hand to help Amy and Ian aboard. "I'll get you out, don't worry. I know every rock and every eddy in that bay. I've got some fellas in the village to help—and some donkeys. They'll block the road. Declan will meet us on the water. Can you cast off that line for me, Danny?"

Dan threw the line in the boat and jumped in. Fiona expertly piloted them through the winding curves of the inlet. "I'll head north and pull in at Runnybeg Creek. It's not on the map and we've just enough draft to make it," she called. "It's just past that turning there."

Before they reached the turning, a boat exploded out of the gray mist, cutting across the inlet straight toward them.

CHAPTER 23

"Hang on!" Fiona shouted, and she jerked the wheel hard to the left. The boat heeled on one side, and she cut across the inlet, skimming between clumps of rocks.

"We're going to have to head for the channel," she shouted. "I can't reverse and get back to Runnybeg now."

Dan looked behind them. The black boat was going slower, no doubt because they didn't have Fiona's knowledge of the inlet. The rocks could tear a hole in the hull. The boat looked like a powerful machine, a dark shark moving through the water. "Are you sure you can outrun them?"

Fiona glanced behind her for a split second, and he saw the doubt flicker on her face. "Possibly not," she said, jerking her chin forward. "But I can outwit them."

As she said this, she suddenly swerved the boat into a narrow channel Dan hadn't noticed. As she followed the twisting channel, she gradually increased her speed, and then the harbor opened up in front of them.

It was just past dawn, and the gray water was still

splashed with pink. The fishing boats were already specks on the far side of the harbor, headed out to deeper water. Fiona zigzagged through the anchored craft, her hands sure and expert on the wheel. The larger boat had trouble following her, so it veered off into the deeper water of the harbor.

"They're going to cut us off!" Amy yelled over the sound of the wind and the water thumping against the hull.

Fiona didn't answer. Her lips pressed together and her eyes narrowed. By slipping through the anchored boats, she began to angle toward shore.

"We'll gain some time when the bay widens," she shouted. "They're too far out to catch us. At least for a bit."

A bit didn't sound too encouraging, Dan thought, but he felt a rush of exhilaration as their boat shot out into open water. Fiona opened up the throttle. The boat slammed down on the waves, and spray drenched their faces.

They were ahead now, and gaining yard after yard. Dan looked behind again. Even though they'd shot ahead, judging by the speed of the other boat it wouldn't be for long. Eventually the other boat would overtake them.

He moved closer to Fiona. "What's the plan?" he asked.

"If I can outrun them and we make it to the cliffs, I can lose them. There's a way."

"The cliffs?"

"The Cliffs of Moher. They lie south of us. If I can get us there fast enough. That's where Declan and his friends will be."

"But how can he help us?"

"HANG ON!" Fiona screamed, suddenly cutting the wheel hard right. The boat heeled up on one side, and Dan dizzily hung on to the cabin rail. He saw a buoy pass inches from his nose.

They were out in the ocean now, the swells impeding their progress. The boat rolled as they cut across the waves, and Dan felt his stomach seize. He kept his eyes on the horizon.

"They're gaining on us," Ian called from the stern.

"I can't get her to go any faster," Fiona said through gritted teeth. "We're almost there."

Then the sun broke through the mist and fog, and through the faint rays they saw the cliffs rise before them, majestic and touched with morning light. Seabirds dove and wheeled above them.

"Whoa," Dan called. "Those are some insane cliffs! What are they, a thousand feet up?"

"Almost . . . the tallest is more like seven hundred," Fiona said, glancing behind her at the black boat. "It's our only chance—they'll be on us in a minute or two. But we'll have company on the water, at least. The Aileens are running. Lucky for us, if we can manage not to sink."

Dan pictured a team of Irish girls running along a cliff. Why would that help them?

"Who are the Aileens?" Amy asked.

"*Aill Na Searrach.* It's a perfect wave," Fiona said. "If conditions are right, and today they are, they can get as big as thirty, forty feet."

"Did you say *forty feet*?" Ian yelled.

"What are those islands out there?" Amy asked, pointing toward massive hills ahead of them.

Dan saw Fiona grip the wheel harder. "Those aren't islands. They're waves."

Dan squinted into the distance. They didn't look like waves. They looked like distant islands that slowly moved across the surface until they grew into massive walls of water.

The boat pursuing them swung off to the left, edging them closer to shore. Closer to the Aileens.

"I won't be able to hold the boat in that surf!" Fiona yelled. "We'll break up! And if I go out to sea, they'll overtake us!"

Dan could see the figures on the deck, the men dressed in black with black sunglasses. He recognized one, a short man with a blond buzz cut in a tight T-shirt. He was the man who'd held him on the bridge. The man raised a rifle.

"Get down!" Dan screamed.

Fiona didn't move. A bullet smashed into the instrument board, cracking the speedometer. Dan crawled over and yanked Fiona down. She kept one hand on the wheel.

"Are you crazy?"

Her face was white, and her teeth chattered. "I didn't think they'd actually *shoot*!" She looked at the torn-up dashboard. "With real *bullets*!"

"Just stay down," Dan ordered.

"If I can't see, I can't steer!" she shouted. "We'll either smash into the rocks or get swept into the surf, and that will be the end of us!"

Dan glanced back. "I think that's what they're going for," he answered.

The men stood, the rifles held loosely in their hands. He could feel the boat groan as it bucked against the swell. If they allowed Fiona to steer, there was no doubt that she would be killed. But if they didn't steer, they'd drift straight into those thirty-foot waves ahead, or into the rocks.

There was a huge tearing noise, and the boat shuddered. "We've hit something!" Fiona shouted. "Ian, can you go below?"

Ian bent over and crab-walked to the cabin as another spray of bullets thudded into the boat. He swung himself down the ladder.

A moment later he stuck his head out. "It's bad," he yelled. "We hit a rock, and there's water pouring in."

"They'll pick us off if we jump in the water," Fiona said. She was still pale, but she was no longer shaking. Her chin was set as she scanned the bay behind them.

"Where are you, Declan, you eejit?" Her voice broke as she searched frantically behind the boat.

Amy crawled forward to sit with Dan, their backs against the cabin door. The boat was now listing to one side. Another wave pummeled them, and they slid a little farther toward the railing. It wouldn't be long now before the boat broke up. The men on the other boat held their rifles, waiting for them to land in the cold water.

"Fiona," she said.

Dan knew what she meant. Another innocent. Another life they'd placed in danger.

"I have to make sure she makes it," Amy said. "So you—just swim. Swim as fast as you can. The water will be cold. You need to keep your muscles warm. Take Olivia's book. And don't look back for me. I'll stay with Fiona. I'll get her to shore."

Dan looked at the roiling water. The rocks. The sheer cliffs. It would be a miracle if they could make it to shore. But he had no intention of swimming for it without making sure Amy was okay. Less than an hour ago he'd been furious at her. Now he'd do anything to save her.

"Piece of cake," he said.

"There they are!" Fiona burst out.

Dan squinted against the sun. Small dark shapes were moving quickly, flying over the surface of the water . . . Jet Skis. Each of them held a pilot and passenger, and each of them were towing something long and sleek. . . .

"Surfboards?" Dan asked.

"It's Declan and his crew," Fiona said. "The Jet Skis tow them behind the peak of the wave, and they ride it in. They're the few mad enough to surf Aileens."

"They *surf* those waves?" Ian said, incredulous.

The Jet Skis veered and came straight toward them. The path would take them right between their boat and the black shark boat. The men on the boat quickly stowed their rifles.

They zoomed closer, forming a wedge and making straight for their boat.

One of the surfers raised a megaphone. "Need help over here?"

"Yes!" Fiona shouted, standing and waving. The Jet Skis surrounded the boat. The men on the other boat wouldn't dare shoot now.

Declan sat on the back of a Jet Ski, dressed in a wet suit. "Looks like you could use a lift," he yelled. He gestured to the surfers perched on the back of the Jet Skis. "These are my mates Sean, Rory, and Patrick. Climb aboard."

"You first, Fiona," Amy said. She hesitated, then thrust Olivia's book into Fiona's hands. "Take care of this."

"I'll take a ride with Sean, there," Fiona said, indicating a red-haired boy with bright blue eyes that were fastened on Fiona. "He'll take me back to the beach at Doolin. I'll take your packs; we've got storage under the seat." In just a moment, the backpacks and Olivia's book were stowed away.

"Is that where you'll take us?" Dan asked as he climbed aboard behind Declan.

"Can't. The boat would just follow you in and pick you off when you dock," Declan said. "And there's fellas on shore at Doolin, waiting. You're going to have to get to shore a different way."

Amy slid off the boat behind Rory. With a grimace, Ian sat behind Patrick. They rocked in the water for a moment as the boat tilted over. Water poured onto the deck.

"You owe me a boat, Fee!" Declan shouted to his sister, grinning.

Dan lurched backward as the Jet Ski took off. He was glad to be leaving the bad guys in the dust, but it would help if at the moment he wasn't heading toward a set of thirty-foot waves.

"Are you taking us to the beach?" he yelled into Declan's ear.

Declan pointed to a wave as high as a building. "Only one way to get there, mate. The Jet Skis can't maneuver in those waves."

"We're going to"—Dan swallowed—"surf in?"

"You'll be on the beach in less than three minutes!" Declan yelled. "All you have to do is hold on."

The Jet Ski sliced through the water. They were now past the break. The Jet Ski rose on the high swell, then skied downhill on the other side. When it hit the trough, Dan felt the thud in his bones.

"They come in sets of seven," Declan yelled. "We're

going to swing in behind the peak. See the barrel shape? 'Tis a beautiful thing. We're going to shoot right inside one of those."

Dan swallowed. He was shaking from cold and fear. He glanced back at Amy. She gave him a shaky thumbs-up. Ian just looked determined and terrified at the same time.

The boy piloting the Jet Ski looked out at the ocean. Apparently, he saw something Dan couldn't. "Here we go! Next set!"

The Jet Skis idled now, and they could hear each other.

"Time to get on the boards," Declan said.

Gingerly, Dan maneuvered himself onto the board. Declan told him how to hold on. Dan's teeth were chattering so loudly he could hear the constant irregular rhythm.

"Won't be long now, mate," Declan said. "Just a minute or two."

Dan looked over. Ian and Amy were on the boards as well.

"No time to waste," Patrick shouted, pointing with his chin at the black boat. They could just make out the men standing on the deck, still watching them. One of them had binoculars trained on them.

Now Dan could see the swell of the wave, like an enormous leviathan moving through the water.

"When it's over the reef, it will start to break," Declan said.

"Let's go!" the Jet Ski pilot called, and they shot forward at top speed. Declan rose gracefully, his feet spread on the board, balancing easily as they sliced through the water. They angled into the forming wave. Dan felt his body crouching on the board like a frozen thing, his mind screaming one word.

Noooooooooo!

Then the wall of water roared toward them and the board shot forward.

CHAPTER 24

Dan's stomach dropped as the power of the wave picked them up and hurtled them forward. He was at the mercy of a force so huge it seemed to suck the air from his lungs, and his head was filled with a booming, primal energy that pushed thought out of his brain and made him pulse with pure feeling.

They shot through a green icy tube of water. He guessed he was screaming, but the roar of the surf was too big around him and holding the slippery board was too hard. Declan's every shift of weight caused another jolt of pure terror to shoot through him.

Through the tunnel of water he could see another surfer ahead, Amy clutching the board. They were parallel to shore, surfing down the curve. Dan could feel the power of the collapsing wave behind them.

"Hang on, we're going to turn!" Declan shouted.

As if he could hang on any more than he was! Declan shifted his body, and the board turned in toward shore. Dan blinked the spray out of his eyes.

Ahead, the other surfer had done the same. He saw Amy sliding across the board, and then she tumbled off, into the churning surf!

He didn't hesitate. He rolled off the board, into the icy water.

Immediately, he felt the fury of the wave, and he struggled to keep his head above the swirling foam. He was like a stick bobbing in its propulsive force. The wave was like an animal, something alive that could easily snap his body in two.

He tensed his body, holding it straight, picking up the pulse of the great wave. He would drown if he got caught in the roiling sea. He had to keep going, find Amy somewhere in the wave.

Ahead, he caught a glimpse of brown — seaweed? No, Amy's hair, streaming out behind her! She, too, was trying to bodysurf the wave. Declan was trying to slow his board, trying to keep Amy in sight.

The minutes seemed forever. The salt stung Dan's eyes and he could no longer feel his fingers. He could see the beach ahead, and he reached out for Amy, trying to grab her foot, or her clothing. . . .

The wave exploded around him, roaring, crashing, and he felt the drag of the receding wave pulling him backward, but he fought to stay up, stay ahead, swimming now for his life, swimming toward Amy. . . .

Who was now flailing, her arms in her heavy wool

sweater dragging her down under the wave. Dan dove straight down. The pull of the wave receded, and he could just make out the pale form of Amy's fluttering hand.

He swam deeper, reaching out, reaching for that hand. And grasped it.

He tugged her forward, swimming until he thought his heart would burst in his chest. He hooked his arm around her and pushed up, up toward the faint light.

He broke through the surface, gasping, and Declan was there, astride his board, his face anguished. He reached down and dragged Dan and Amy over his board. Then he paddled to shore.

The other surfers and Ian came running. Together, they got Dan and Amy on the beach. Amy doubled over, coughing.

Declan sat, his head between his knees, his whole body shuddering. His cocky attitude was wiped away by near disaster.

Dan lay on the beach, trying to catch his breath.

Amy looked up through her tangle of wet hair. "Saved my life again, bro," she said raggedly. "I owe you two."

Up above, Sean and Fiona ran down the cliff's switch-back trail, their arms full of blankets. Amy tried to struggle to her feet. No doubt her knees were just as liquid as Dan's. Ian shook sand out of his trouser pockets.

"Declan, we've got to move," Patrick said. "We've only got a few minutes before they call to shore and tell them we'll be coming up the cliffs."

"Right." Declan stood, tossing his dark hair out of his eyes.

The black boat was just a dot in the distance, heading back the way it came.

Dan realized he was freezing, shaking so badly he was having trouble walking. Fiona ran down the beach and threw a blanket around Amy, then Dan. "Come on," she urged. "There's no time."

They followed the surfers up the path to a caravan of vehicles. Declan led the way to his truck. He opened the doors for them. "I'll be back in a tick," he said, and then disappeared into the van parked next to them.

They fell into the truck, shivering. Fiona passed in a thermos and cups. "This is nice and hot; it will warm you up. Declan will drive you to the airport. There's a private plane there. Here's the number of the pilot. He'll take you anywhere you need to go." Her blue eyes were fierce. "You'll be safe, I promise you. Declan can drive like the devil and he knows these back roads like nobody else."

"He surfs like the devil, too," Dan said. The shaking was coming under control.

Declan reappeared, now dressed in jeans and a thick wool sweater, his hair slicked back. He slid behind the wheel.

"Good-bye, Fiona," Amy said. "Thank you for everything. That's not nearly enough to say, but . . ."

"Don't worry," Fiona said. "We'll meet again. I'm sure of it." She shut the door, then gave the truck a pat.

Declan hit the gas and they took off, spraying dirt as they peeled out of the lot.

It wasn't until they were halfway to the Dublin airport that they warmed up completely and Amy felt her brain beginning to work again.

"How did they find us?" she wondered. "We haven't used our phones for e-mail. We hardly left the house in the past two days. . . ."

"Except for Ian," Dan said. "Did you notice anything suspicious when you went for your walk?"

Ian shook his head. "No surveillance. I would have seen it. Just me and my bike. Of course, I almost got run over, but that was an accident."

"Accident?" Amy asked sharply.

"My bike met the fender of a Range Rover," Ian said. "Lucky for me I wasn't on it at the time. The driver gave me a ride as far as Ballycreel."

Amy was instantly suspicious. "What was her name?"

"How do you know it was a girl?"

"Because if I was going to try to put a track on us through you, I'd use a girl to do it," Amy answered.

"Her name was Maura, and she wasn't some spy, she was a very lovely and very rich young woman in her daddy's expensive car, and she gave me a very short ride over some very bumpy fields to the nearest village," Ian said huffily. "End of story."

"How did the accident happen?" Dan asked.

"I don't appreciate being cross-examined," Ian said. "I'm a Lucian. I know what I'm doing. I didn't tell the girl my real name. I made sure she was gone before I walked back to Bhaile Anois."

"Did this girl ask to use your phone?" Amy asked.

"No. It was never out of my possession. Except . . ." Ian suddenly stopped. His face went red. "Except when she hit the bicycle, I dove for cover, and the phone flew out of my hands. . . ."

"And she picked it up." Amy held out her hand. "Let me see your phone."

"This is ridiculous!" Nevertheless, Ian sighed and dug in his leather backpack. He handed his phone to Amy. The words KEEP CALM AND CARRY ON mocked him from the cover.

Amy turned on the phone. She looked at it, then handed it back. "You have to input your code."

With a roll of his eyes, Ian typed in his number code.

```
WRONG PASSCODE
Try Again
```

Ian typed it in again.

```
WRONG PASSCODE
Try Again
```

He turned the phone around in his hands. "This isn't my phone! It's all scuffed and scratched." He looked up. "Jake must have taken my phone by mistake."

Thoughts tumbled in Amy's head. It all made sense. "She put a tracker on your phone," she said. "That's how they tracked us to the area. But Jake took your phone by mistake this morning. That means they're now tracking *him.*"

Amy quickly dialed Ian's cell number. Ian's voice came on the line. "You've reached me. Leave a message. Don't make it tedious. Good-bye."

"He's not picking up," Amy said frantically. "If there's a tracker on his phone, Pierce and his men know where he is. They'll go after him and Atticus!"

CHAPTER 25

Attleboro, Massachusetts

Nellie had discovered something about Pony: He was more docile if he was fed.

She could easily whip up a five-course French meal, but Pony preferred the basics. Her grilled cheese made him swoon. Especially when she made him her home-made potato chips, roasted with olive oil and sea salt.

"Much healthier for you, dude," she told him.

She'd fed him dinner and snacks for days now. He didn't seem much closer to giving her what she wanted: a secure digital network. Still, he was a genius. And it was hard to get completely annoyed at someone who had nicknamed her "goddess."

Pony groaned as he scooped up the last bite of spaghetti carbonara. He picked up the rest of his crumbs of garlic bread with a moistened index finger. Then he leaned back, closed his eyes, and belched.

Still with his eyes closed, he said, "In some cultures,

that is a compliment. Though I'm not certain that's actually true."

"If I had Internet access, I could look it up," Nellie said pointedly, clearing his plate.

"Whoa. I am operating at full maximum," he protested. "This hackitude is off the charts. It's *April May* we're talking about," he added, lowering his voice the way he always did when he spoke of the hacker. "She — or he — is the supreme ghostnetting empress of all time. She's hacked into AT&T, federal agencies, the government of Bulgaria . . . even *Disney World*! I can't clear your network until I know it's totally protected. You understand? It has to be a *fortress of impregnability.*"

She set out a bowl of homemade butterscotch ice cream, his favorite, but she held the spoon in the air. "I can't keep running to random Internet cafés, and neither can Amy and Dan. We need phones!"

"Well, since I cannot disappoint my lady, I will give you a present." Pony reached into one of his enormous pockets and brought out a pile of smartphones. "Your own personal fortress of Cahill impregnability. And, if all goes well, I'll have a laptop for you later on tonight. Now that I know who I'm dealing with, I've been able to ensure that these are safe. And I'll be totally monitoring at all times. Now can I have the spoon?"

Nellie handed it to him, then hugged the phone. "Where have you been all my life?" she crooned to it.

Pony snickered. "I've been playing a cat-and-mouse

game with April May. Except it's invisible cat, invisible mouse. She doesn't know that I've managed a way in. I am spying on her, too. I found her back door and used it. A small breach she will never discover, but enough to tell me things. I am closer than close to making us a fortress indeed." Pony eyed the pitcher of hot fudge sauce Nellie had placed on the table. "And if you pass that pitcher, I will reveal a nugget of information that will please you and instantly return me to your good goddess graces."

Nellie pushed the pitcher forward. "Spill. Not the fudge sauce. The info."

"While I have been diligently working on fortressing up your network, I have had a few minutes of downtime in which I trolled around for your other request."

Nellie leaned forward. "You found out something about Pierce."

"Indeed." Pony took a heaping spoonful of ice cream. "In addition to snatching up media companies right and left, our Malevolent Malefactor, J. Rutherford Pierce, has, under a variety of shell companies, bought a pharmaceutical research lab right outside of Wilmington, Delaware—"

"Delaware!" Nellie exclaimed.

"—and fired its employees." With the spoon in his mouth, he fished into his pocket and extracted a piece of paper. He pushed it across the table to Nellie. "Here's the address."

"Why would he buy . . ." Dread invaded Nellie, a

slow realization that took her breath. "How big is the lab, Pony?"

"Big outfit. They used to manufacture lots of drugs. Cold remedies. And everybody gets colds!"

"So the infrastructure is there. . . ." Nellie swallowed. She chewed on her lip. "It could be . . . it really could. It makes sense."

"Waiting for you to download on me, goddess."

"Amy was right. Those thugs who came after them . . . their strength. Their power. It's not just Pierce who took the serum! He took Sammy's work and he . . . he used it to create those hyperstrong henchmen. There's a *reason* he bought that lab."

Pony stared at her, uncomprehending.

"He's going to manufacture the serum! He's planning on *mass-producing* it! Why else would he buy a lab?"

"And that would be bad?"

Nellie stood up and paced. "It would be *catastrophic*. He could do anything! Create an army of supermen. Squads of tactical leaders. All under his control. Because he'd be controlling the serum. Don't you see? He can make the most powerful army in the world! If he's the one to decide, if he's the one to control who gets it . . . he could create a whole network of Piercers. People strong enough and clever enough to do anything. With no scruples. People who would kill kids without even blinking an eye. Terror would be part of daily life. The rest of us would just be . . ."

"His sock puppets," Pony finished.

"Sammy is there," Nellie declared. "I know it. Pierce wouldn't get rid of him. He'd *use* him. Sammy is the one who laid the groundwork. Now he has to finish what he started."

Nellie whirled around. "I've got to pack . . . find surveillance equipment . . ."

"Nellie? One more thing." Pony stood up. "In the course of tricking April May, I made a discovery. WALDO has hacked into the CCTV system in London. You know, the closed-circuit TV system that Scotland Yard uses? And Amy and Dan are on their way there."

"London? Are you saying that Pierce could track them through the CCTV?"

"It's tough, but possibly doable, with the right program. But basically? Yeah."

She looked down at the new smartphones on the table, thinking hard. "We have to get these to them," she declared. "But I can't ship them. I don't trust anything anymore."

"You could hop a flight, get them to the kids personally," Pony said with a shrug.

She looked up at Pony. "Or you could."

"Me?"

"You. I can't leave now, Pony. And you could check out the Rosenbloom brothers' phones, too. You have to make sure the whole system is secure."

"I can't just pick up and go," Pony said. "I have a cat."

"You can bring the cat here. I have a cat-sitter. The best in the world—my mom. She loves cats."

"I can't fly. I'm allergic to peanuts."

"I made you peanut butter cookies on Monday because you said they were your favorite."

"I don't have a suitcase."

"I'll loan you one. Pony, I *need* you," Nellie said. "The *world* needs you."

"Me? No. You don't understand, Nellie." Pony's soft brown eyes were full of a new expression—fear. "I've never *been* anywhere. I mean, aside from virtually."

Nellie snapped her fingers. "Wait a second—I finally got through to Jonah Wizard. You can fly with him on his private plane."

"J-Jonah Wizard?" Pony stammered. "The *star*?"

"He's also a Cahill. Amy and Dan's cousin." Nellie finally noticed the look of absolute terror on Pony's face at the thought of meeting a world-famous hip-hop artist. She smiled. Jonah had all the trappings of a star—the private plane, the bling, the 'tude—but underneath it all, he was a nice guy.

"Don't worry," she reassured Pony. "He's nice. He's due into Logan in"—Nellie checked her watch—"two hours. Then you can both fly to London. You can do this, Pony."

"I guess . . ."

She put a hand on his sleeve. "Here's the thing. If you've never been anywhere, isn't it time to start?"

He gulped. "If you say so."

Twenty minutes later, Pony arrived at her house with a paper bag full of clothes and his cat in a carrier. Nellie gave him a backpack. She had already packed him a sandwich, cookies, and an apple. Pony felt like a kindergartner, but he was grateful that Nellie had agreed to walk him through the terror.

And then he'd have to be alone with the fantastic Jonah Wizard. For *hours.* He was sure he'd say something idiotic.

Nellie ducked into the security room to set the code. Pony stood outside, shifting from one foot to another. Did private planes have security lines? Would he have to take off his shoes? He couldn't remember if he had a hole in his sock. He felt like a total loser. This was exactly why he didn't participate in real life! It was too real!

He reached over and lifted the mailbox flap. There was some junk mail, but there was also a small manila envelope addressed to Amy Cahill. He stuffed it into his bag. He was probably going to botch everything. Whenever he participated in real life, things went wrong. But the least he could do was bring Amy Cahill her mail.

CHAPTER 26

London, England

The trouble with the United States of America was, it had never had a dictator. All those pesky senators, the courts, the judges, the *people* — by them, for them . . . It just mucked up the works.

Pierce turned, irritated, as Debi Ann came into the room. She still looked tired from jet lag. She didn't have his stamina. Early on, he had made the decision not to give her the serum adaptations. After all, each serum was calibrated according to the desired result. He, of course, got the most powerful dose. As for Debi Ann, America needed a member of his family to identify with: someone non-fabulous, unlike himself and his kids. Debi Ann's very ordinariness was going to help sweep him into the White House.

Still . . .

He glanced at himself in the mirror, then at her. It was undeniable that he was looking younger, and she was looking older.

She peered into the mirror behind him, adjusting the sweep of her blond hair so that it hit her chin at the right angle. "I'm going to do some shopping this morning, dear," she said.

"Mm-hmm."

"Sometimes I think the British appreciate teddy bears more than we do, I am sad to say. . . ."

Pierce tried to stifle his annoyance, but he couldn't help himself. "If all goes the way it should, Debi Ann—and it will—you really have to find another cause. I mean, really. *Teddy bears?* Can't you find an interest that's more . . . first ladyish?"

Debi Ann stiffened. "They aren't teddy bears, they are *icons.* Symbols of the innocence of childhood. Quality toys for quality kids," she said, repeating the slogan of her Save the Teddies group. "It's about conserving our cultural toy heritage. And our children's *health*, dear. Don't get me started on polyfill."

No, he did not want to get her started on polyfill.

Debi Ann kept on talking, but Pierce lost the thread of her conversation. What he did not foresee after he boosted his Lucian quotient was how boring he'd suddenly find his wife. Too late to change now, though.

Pierce looked at himself in the mirror again. *Actually . . .*

Once he was in office . . . a little sympathy for a grieving widower went a long way, didn't it?

CHAPTER 27

As soon as they landed and were taxiing to the terminal, Jake's phone rang. An unfamiliar number came up in caller ID.

Amy answered it nervously. To her great relief, it was Nellie.

"Amy, is that you? Why are you on Jake's phone?"

"He took Ian's phone by mistake. Nellie, I'm afraid they're being tracked!" Amy said frantically.

"Are you in London?"

"We just landed."

"Listen, I don't have much time. I sent Pony with Jonah—they'll meet you at the Greensward Hotel, King's Cross, at three P.M. They'll be delivering new secure phones. I'm driving to Delaware."

"Delaware? What's there?"

"Long story. Sammy is missing, and I'm going to find him. Kiddo, I'm afraid this plan is even bigger than we thought. You were right about his security guys. I think he gave them a special Tomas boost. But I think they're just a test case. He's going to mass-produce it."

Amy felt sick. "Mass-produce it . . . the serum? Are you sure?"

"He just bought a major pharmaceutical lab. That's where I'm headed."

"Alone? You can't . . ."

"Better this way."

"No!"

"I have to go. Stay in touch."

Nellie hung up. Amy quickly filled in Ian and Dan.

"Mass-produce the serum . . ." Ian said. "That can't . . ."

". . . happen," Dan finished. "It would be . . ."

"Unthinkable," Amy said. "He could make an *army* of those guys."

"An invincible force," Ian said. "Undefeatable."

"And now they could be after Atticus and Jake." Amy tried to call Ian's number again, praying that Jake would pick up.

Please pick up, Jake. Please . . .

When she heard his voice, she collapsed back against the seat. "Jake, it's Amy."

"Amy, what is it?" Jake's tone was frosty.

"Listen fast, because I think there's a GPS tracker on your phone. You have Ian's phone and he has yours. Where are you now?"

"Heading for our hotel. We couldn't get a flight out until tomorrow morning."

"Did you pay for the hotel with a credit card?"

"Yes . . ."

199

"Don't go there. They could be waiting. They could be following you now. There's a hotel near King's Cross station called the Greensward. Stay with crowds, walk around, and meet us there in a half hour."

"I don't understand—"

"Ditch the phone after we hang up. We can't be sure, Pierce might want to take out our friends, too. And that means you and Atticus. *Just make sure you're not followed.*" Amy hung up before Jake could protest.

Amy, Dan, and Ian hurried off the plane and into the terminal. They passed a newsstand on the way to the escalator. The headline screamed at them.

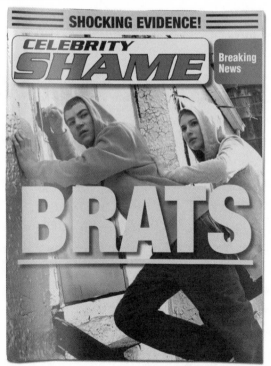

SHOCKING EVIDENCE!

CELEBRITY SHAME

Breaking News

BRATS

It was splashed over a picture of Amy and Dan.

"Oh, no," Amy breathed, stopping short. "Not here, too!"

Another paper shouted:

THEY NEED A NANNY.

And, the worst one: a picture of Ian, looking handsome in a blazer and tie.

JUST ANOTHER HOTTIE, OR IS IT TRUE LOVE AT LAST FOR AMY?

Amy groaned.

"I hate that photo," Ian said. "It was my school picture. The fit of that blazer is simply horrendous."

A woman eyed her, then whispered to her companion, who stared. "Let's get out of here," Amy muttered. "It'll be even easier for Pierce to find us if the paparazzi are after us!"

Ian looked at his watch. "I hate to succumb to public transport, but the Tube will be faster. Follow me."

They dashed through the terminal, up escalators, and into people movers until they got to the platform. Amy gazed down it, her nerves screaming.

If anything happens to them, I'll . . .

I don't know what I'll do . . .

Ian touched her arm. "I'm sorry. I made the most elementary, stupid mistake a Cahill could make. I trusted a stranger."

Amy gazed at him without seeing him. Was that what being a Cahill was? Being afraid to trust a helpful stranger? Always paranoid, always watchful, never trusting? Always looking for the bad, not the good?

If that's true, I don't want to be a Cahill anymore, either, she thought suddenly, looking over at Dan. He was gazing down the tunnel and then at his watch, his foot tapping nervously.

"No, Ian," she said. "It wasn't your fault. We're not superheroes. We're just kids, Ian. Just kids."

Jake stared down at Ian's phone. It felt like it was burning his fingers. He wanted to drop it in the nearest trash can, but that impulse wouldn't help them.

"Was that Amy, Jake? Did she change her mind?" Atticus hopped on one foot, then the other.

"No . . ." Jake said.

He didn't want to scare his younger brother. They were now on a busy commercial street with lots of shops with plate-glass windows. Like mirrors. They could help him. Jake stopped at a shop window. Behind him he could see the steady stream of pedestrians. Just people strolling, or hurrying to an appointment. Tourists ambling, looking for souvenirs to take back home.

"I took Ian's phone by mistake," Jake said. "She wanted to let me know."

"Oh," Atticus said in a small voice. "Does she want to see us?"

"We're supposed to meet them at their hotel."

"Woo-hoo!" Atticus said. "Maybe she *did* change her mind!"

Jake was now hyperaware of his surroundings. Every time he passed a window, he used it to check behind them. He needed to stop and see if that would flush out anyone.

Ahead of them, several fashionable women walked, holding shopping bags and chatting.

Jake tugged on Atticus's arm. "Look, it's a bookshop up ahead." It was the only diversion that would halt Atticus. "Let's check it out." He quickly swiveled toward the shop, brushing by the women. As he did, he dropped the phone into one of their shopping bags.

"They have old books!" Atticus jogged toward the entrance.

A man in jeans and a black jacket walked past them, then paused outside a pub and checked his watch, as if he were waiting for someone.

"Can we go in? Do we have time?" Atticus asked.

"Sure," Jake said.

They pushed through the door and Atticus headed to the shelves marked CLASSICAL LITERATURE. Jake stood by the window. From this angle he could see the man still standing in front of the pub. The man wore an earpiece, the wire sneaking inside his jacket, and Jake saw his mouth moving.

Could be just a guy, talking on the phone.

But something about the coiled assurance of how he stood . . .

Jake scanned the sidewalk across the street. With a sinking feeling, he saw another man across the street. A man in dark clothes, waiting for a bus. Except the bus just left, and he didn't get on.

Jake drifted toward Atticus. "Att? We've got to split. Out the back door. And then we have to run. Some very large men are right outside, looking for us."

Atticus's eyes were wide. "We're being followed?"

Jake nodded. "We've got to lose these guys. We can't lead them to Amy and Dan. Come on."

Atticus and Jake walked toward the rear of the shop, surprising a clerk with a stack of books.

"Excuse me, gentlemen? This is a private area—"

"My brother is sick. Does this door go outside—"

Atticus made a convincing gagging sound.

The clerk took a step back. "The alley. Oh, my, yes, go right ahead."

"Where does it go?"

"It will bring you to Oxford Street—"

Jake pushed the door open, shielding Atticus. The alley was empty.

The alley ran past the shops, then turned right. Jake and Atticus jogged down it. After the turn they could see Oxford Street ahead, the busiest street in London. Jake thought fast. There would be even more people there, and buses. Lots of buses.

They had almost reached the end when Jake heard the sound of running footsteps. He turned and saw the man from outside the pub. He'd already covered half the distance of the alley. He was *fast.*

"Run," Jake said.

They burst onto Oxford Street. Jake saw a bus just pulling up across the street.

"Stay with me, buddy." He darted into the traffic, holding up his hand to stop the cars. Horns blared.

"Sorry!" Jake shouted. "Stupid American tourist!"

He and Atticus weaved through the traffic. "Hold the bus!" Jake shouted.

Someone yelled, "Are you daft, you two?"

They landed safely on the opposite sidewalk. Behind him, Jake could see two men trying to weave through traffic. One vaulted over a car.

Over a car?

Jake didn't have time to think. The bus was just taking off as he lifted his skinny brother and placed him on the step, then jumped aboard, grabbing the rail and pulling himself up.

Atticus hung on to the rail, panting, but grinning in relief. Jake looked behind. The man was running along the sidewalk, trying to keep up with the bus, but he ran into a crowd of tourists and the bus turned the corner. Safe.

Not for long. Because now they were a target, too.

CHAPTER 28

Text from April May to J. Rutherford Pierce, routed to Security 1:

CCTV shows targets passing through
Kings Cross station. Picked up again on
Euston Rd. Lost somewhere btwn Euston
and Pancras station. Four hotels in two-
block area. Suggest ground search.

Pony was surrounded by scones, whipped cream, jam, and cake when Amy, Dan, and Ian caught up to him in the Greensward Hotel restaurant. Jonah lounged nearby, his famous face obscured by a slouchy cap and tinted glasses. He jumped up when he saw them.

"My homeys!" Jonah hugged Amy and bumped Dan's and Ian's fists. He gestured at Pony. "This is his second tea. He digs clotted cream."

Though Jonah's words were light, Amy could see

how relieved he was to see them. Pony jumped up, wiping his mouth, and they introduced him to Ian.

They pulled up chairs, but Amy anxiously kept her eye on the lobby doors. Jonah had chosen well. They were on a balcony overlooking the lobby, with views in all directions. From here, they could go down the stairs to the main entrance, or take a side entrance down a short corridor. The lobby was thronged with tourists, but the restaurant was half empty. They had privacy, and yet a full view. Perfect.

"Let's bust out the new tech, son," Jonah said to Pony.

Pony grinned with pride and slid new smartphones across the table. "These are totally fortress-safe. Encryption, et cetera — your basic moats and barbed wire and electric fences. A program will constantly run security checks. I'll put the same thing on Atticus's and Jake's phones."

"This is Jake's phone," Amy said, pushing it over. "They should be here soon." She crossed her fingers underneath the table. She knew it was a childish gesture, but she was too anxious to care.

Ian and Dan quickly filled Jonah and Pony in on what they had discovered in Ireland.

Amy felt too nervous to listen. She uncrossed her fingers and checked her watch. Where *were* they? If anything happened to Jake and Atticus . . .

Then suddenly there they were, hurrying through the doors into the lobby. Amy felt sweet relief pour through her. She wanted to jump up and shout, but instead she waited quietly until Jake's gaze moved around the lobby, then up to the balcony. She lifted her hand.

They climbed the stairs quickly and joined them at the table. "Were you followed?" Amy asked.

"We lost them," Jake said, sitting down. He tossed a newspaper on the table. Amy winced when she saw the TRUE LOVE AT LAST headline about her and Ian, but Jake just flipped the paper over to point to another headline. PRESIDENT PIERCE? A photo of J. Rutherford Pierce shaking hands with an uneasy-looking prime minister dominated the page.

"I read the article. Pierce is on his goodwill tour, and it's going to end at a press conference on his island in Maine. In two weeks. It's expected that he's going to announce that he's running for president. He's throwing this huge clambake for his supporters."

"That might be the perfect opportunity to slip him the antidote," Amy said. "He'll be mingling, shaking hands, eating and drinking. . . ."

"Good plan," Dan said. "Except that we don't have the antidote. We haven't cracked the code yet."

"Or discovered the formula," Jonah said.

"Or gathered the ingredients," Ian said.

"Let's hope there's not thirty-nine," Amy said, and they smiled ruefully at each other. Amy looked into Jake's eyes. He quickly glanced away.

"Two weeks? No problem," Atticus said. "Let's get started."

Pony looked up from his cream puff. "You dudes are awesome," he said.

Nellie had booked them a hotel room, just in case. Pony loped downstairs to the lobby to pick up the key. They all piled onto elevators to the fourteenth floor and set up camp. They moved the desk to the middle of the room and put Olivia's book on it with a pile of paper and pencils.

Amy watched as Atticus kicked off his sneakers and sharpened a pencil. Jake pored over the book. He hadn't looked at her once. He would never forgive her for kicking him out of the house in Ireland.

In her heart, she vowed that nothing would happen to them. She would die first.

Text Message from Security 1 to Security 3:

```
Surveillance of Renaissance Hotel com-
pleted. Move on to Clarke Hotel Pancras Rd.
```

"'Now take what thee owns outright, count eight and on the sixth do pause. / Take that sixth, match to first that Romans brought' . . . What does she mean, 'what thee owns outright'?" Dan asked.

"I own a plane," Jonah said. "Three cribs. But not outright. One has a mortgage."

Jake smiled wryly at Jonah and gave him a fist bump. "From what Amy's told me, once Olivia Cahill lost the family estate in a fire, they had to make their own way. So if she's talking to her daughter, they might have had nothing at all."

"We own who we are," Dan said. "I mean, basically, when you have nothing, at least you have that." He thumped his chest. "Me, Dan. You, Atticus."

Atticus laughed, but Jake looked at Dan for a long moment. Amy looked at Jake. His gaze slid from her brother to her.

"Her name," they said together.

"'That which you own outright' is her *name*," Amy explained to the others.

"Madeleine. Nine letters," Jake said.

Amy shook her head. "Can't be, then. Olivia says 'eight.'"

Dan padded over to them in his socks. "'Her Joy, her *Song*,'" he said. "Isn't a madrigal a song?"

"A medieval song without instruments," Jake said. "For four to six voices . . ."

"Olivia had five children," Amy said. "She wanted Madeleine to reunite the family. *Madrigal* could have been a pet name for her!"

"Eight letters," Jake said.

Atticus's pencil was moving quickly. "It's a simple alphabet code!" he burst out. "'Match to first that Romans brought' . . . the Romans brought us the alphabet!"

"Stop on the sixth," Jake said.

"M-A-D-R-I-G," Amy counted. "Start with a G. Match it to first — means —"

Atticus was already working, his pencil flying. "Substitute *G* for *A* as first letter," he muttered. "That means *G* is really *A*, and the next letter, *H*, is really *B*, and so on . . . easy peasy."

He held up the paper. "This is the new alphabet. Now I can really get to work."

G H I J K L
A B C D E F

M N O P Q
G H I J K

R S T U V
L M N O P

W X Y Z
Q R S T

A B C D E
U V W X Y

F
Z

Jake was busy decoding. "Wait . . . there's a null," he told Atticus.

"A null?" Dan asked.

"A cipher term. It's a letter or a number, usually, but it means nothing. It's just thrown in the mix to confuse. This one is just a consecutive letter. Easy to strike out." Jake bent over his page again.

"No *clue* what he means," Pony said, stretching out on the bed, "but he's my hero, man."

"The rest of this is in Italian. Jake—you're better at translating. I'm all about dead languages," Atticus said.

"That's because you're a zombie student of doom," Dan told him.

Atticus stiff-walked across the room at him and they began to zombie-wrestle, but they stopped and drew closer when Jake began to read aloud, translating as he went.

"'After my mother's death, such profound grief we felt that my father decided to journey to the land of his youthful study. At the age of fourteen I traveled first to Milan, where I met the companion of his youth, now the great and famous teacher. He took me on secretly as his apprentice, though I was a girl, after his eye fell upon some drawings and sketches of mine. We studied in secret, and perhaps it was that conspiracy of learning that led us to the deepest friendship of my life.'" Jake looked up. "She calls him *maestro di vita*, just like in the poem. It's Leonardo, of course. She continues that he taught her botany, anatomy, drawing, painting. . . . And then, when she was seventeen, 'My destiny appeared one day at the doorway of the studio. My Gideon.'"

Jake paused, translating as he spoke. "They marry when she's nineteen. There's some kind of dowry. . . ."

"The dowry!" Ian crowed. "I knew it! What was it?"

"'Bequeathed to me by my teacher, who knew Gideon would use it well. *Urbes Perditae Codex*,'" Atticus translated over Jake's shoulder. "The Lost Cities Codex. 'Copied and written herein.'"

Jake dragged a hand through his hair. "This is unbelievable. A lost Leonardo manuscript, transcribed by your ancestor!"

"But what *is* it?" Amy asked. "And what does it have to do with the antidote?"

"Give us a minute," Jake said. He spread out papers on the desk, then consulted the book. Atticus held up a mirror, and together, speaking in low voices, they translated Olivia's pages while Amy paced, Dan stood on his head, Jonah stood at the window, Ian tried to help, and Pony's head drooped and he let out a loud snore.

Finally, Jake put down his pen and ran his hand through his hair again.

Atticus sat back. "Okay. My mind is officially blown."

"Apparently . . ." Jake stopped and took a breath. "This is so hard to grasp . . . but this document given to Olivia is about the great lost civilizations of the world—seven of them. At the very end, they kept their greatest wisdom—their cures, their potions, their medicines—and wrote them down. They were passed to the last survivors, and over years and years they were compiled into one document—which passed from hand to hand to the greatest scholar of the age. Until they finally got to Leonardo da Vinci."

"Who gave it to your ancestor," Atticus told them. "Olivia Behan Cahill."

"So this codex—Olivia copied all the information in her book?" Amy asked.

"To hide it," Jake said. "I'm guessing that each care-taker copied over the information so that it would be easier to keep and pass along."

Amy had memorized the poem by now. She spoke softly. "'. . . and take up battle not with arms but wis-dom gained from ancient land / kept close and passed from hand to hand . . .'"

Dan continued. "'. . . to *mio maestro di vita*, thee of timeless woman, universal man. / Then he to me bequeathed it, and with instruction bid / and I, through his own methods, hid.'"

"'Through his own methods'—that means the mir-ror writing. Leonardo used that, too," Atticus said. "But there's a problem."

"There's *always* a problem, bro," Jonah said. "Welcome to CahillLand."

Jake tapped the table. "From what I've read, the codex is just what it says. Under each civilization there are short texts that give advice, list medicines, even poisons—all sorts of things. It tells you how to cure snakebite, kill an enemy, even induce a coma. But there's nothing here that appears to be added by Olivia. So . . ."

"There's no formula for an antidote," Amy finished.

"At least an obvious formula. There are also numbered lists of ingredients under each civilization," Jake explained. "For example, Carthage has fifteen, Angkor Wat has twenty-two, Tikal has twelve. But—no formula."

"But why would it be in the codex anyway?" Ian asked. "Gideon *used* the secrets in the book to make the serum, and Olivia used them for the antidote. It's got to be in her section of the book."

"But I've read it cover to cover!" Amy exclaimed. "More than once."

"Wait a second," Dan said briskly. "We've figured out what all of the poem means except one line. What about 'with no edges glimpsed, dark sketched the key imparted'?"

"You're right, Dan," Amy agreed excitedly. She turned the pages of the book. "Dark sketched . . . the black pages maybe?" She looked at them, then at the page with the Madrigal *M*.

"Wait a minute," she said. "Olivia said she used Leonardo's own methods, right? Does anyone have a magnifying glass?"

Atticus dug in his pack and came up with one. Amy studied the page with the Madrigal *M* through the magnifying glass. It was a dark, inky page, with the *M* in the center, and twining leaves, herbs, and flowers around it.

"I read up on Leonardo on Jake's phone on the plane," she said. "He worked on the *Mona Lisa* for almost twenty years. Art historians think it's because he used a tiny brush and a magnifying lens. The technique is called *sfumato* — 'Leonardo's smoke.' There are layers and layers and layers to the painting. He didn't want you to see where one color changed to another — the edges."

Amy's face was close to the book now. "I see it!" she cried. "Olivia has hidden letters in the cross-hatching. There's a text that winds around the M. It's concealed in the leaves. You can't see it with the naked eye! I see the word *Carthage* — the lost city. 'Tincture one dram.' And the number eight. Didn't you say the ingredients were numbered, Jake?"

"Hang on." Jake turned the pages of the book. "Number eight in the Carthage section is . . . silphium. Whatever that is."

"Keep going, Amy," Dan said. "What next?"

Amy picked up the magnifying glass again. Working carefully but quickly, she found all seven civilizations, numbers of ingredients, and amounts. Jake wrote them down.

Troy: six whiskers from an Anatolian leopard, ground to a powder
Carthage: silphium, tincture one dram

Tikal: Riven crystal, one dram ground to a powder

Angkor: Venom of a Tonle Sap Water Snake, half
   jigger

Pueblo: one head of ◎

Britannia: copper butterfly wing

Abyssina: boiled roots of three dingetenga plants

"What country is Carthage in?" Dan asked.

"Present-day Tunisia," Atticus answered.

"Angkor is Cambodia," Ian said. "And Tikal?"

"One of the great civilizations of world history,"
Atticus said. "Dates back to the fourth century B.C. You
can tour the ruins in Guatemala."

"There it is," Dan said. "Another worldwide quest.
At least there's only seven civilizations, not thirty-nine.
But where is Troy? I didn't know it was real. I mean, it
was real in the movie, but . . ."

"It was a real place," Jake answered. "The ruins are
in Turkey."

"Maybe we should start there," Amy said. "Turkey
isn't too long a flight from here."

"Six whiskers from a leopard?" Dan asked. "I'm glad
this stuff is so easy. What are we supposed to do, run
after it with a pair of tweezers?"

Jake frowned over his laptop. "Wait. I've got some
bad news. Silphium is a plant used in classical antiq-
uity. It is extinct. So is the Anatolian leopard."

"Oh, man," Jonah said from the floor, where he was
reclining, a pillow under his head. "That is messed up."

"How can we make a potion from things that don't exist anymore?" Ian asked.

The mood in the room instantly flattened. It felt as though the chase was over before it had begun.

"Hey, bros," Jonah said, leaping to his feet in the smooth move that earned him the title of most viewed music video of all time. "Just because it's messed up doesn't mean we can't fix the prob. We found thirty-nine *clues*, homeys. We can locate some *whiskers*."

"Jonah's right. We can't take no for an answer," Amy declared. "I say we go to Turkey and see what we can find. And we'll figure out silphium, too, when the time comes. We don't have a choice. We have to try."

"YOLO," Jonah agreed. The rest of them looked puzzled. "Explain, dawg," Jonah said, pointing at Pony.

"You Only Live Once," Pony translated.

"Precisely," Ian said. "If we go and explore, we'll find a way."

"And the best thing we can do right now," Jake said, "is get out of London."

"Plane fueled up and ready to go, bro," Jonah said. "Next stop, Istanbul."

Text from Security 1 to Security 3:

```
Clarke Hotel clear. Next search:
Greensward Hotel.
```

CHAPTER 29

They all piled into the elevators for the trip to the lobby. The first one was full, and somehow in the confusion Amy found herself in an elevator alone with Jake.

They stood in uncomfortable silence. It was now or never. Amy gathered her courage. She couldn't go on like this, with Jake avoiding her eyes.

She stepped forward and punched every floor on the way down.

"What are you doing?" Jake demanded.

"I want to talk to you alone, and I have a feeling this is my only chance." Amy paused. The elevator doors opened on an empty hallway, then closed.

"I'm sorry," she said. "I'm sorry you're involved in all this."

"Right," Jake said, his eyes on the floor indicator. "I remember. We're not family."

"Well, yes. Why should you sacrifice everything for us?"

"If you don't know the answer to that, forget it."

The doors opened on a tourist couple. "Sorry!"

Amy trilled, and punched at the DOOR CLOSE button.

"You don't understand," Amy started.

Jake broke in furiously. "I think I do. Last fall we were under a pressure situation, we got too close, now we're back to reality. You feel differently now."

"I just think," Amy said carefully, "that if we could just stay friends . . . it would be great. Because we have a lot of work to do, and if you can't even look me in the eye, it could compromise our mission."

The doors opened to an empty hallway, then closed.

"Oh, so now I'm a security risk," Jake said bitterly.

"That's not what I meant! I don't want Atticus to be in danger. You still have a chance to leave. If you go back to Rome—"

"They *saw* us, Amy! For all I know they have a whole *dossier* by now. We're in this, whether you like it or not. My only hope for protecting my brother is to *stop Pierce.* Just like it's your only way to protect Dan."

The doors opened on a businessman. He started forward, saw their stormy faces, and said, "I'll wait for the next one."

"Anyway, you're right," Jake said as the door closed again. "The mission is most important. I get it now. If you've got some ancient docs to decode, I'm your man. But when it comes to actually *needing* someone . . . well, you'd rather take a pass."

"How I *feel* isn't important right now. Feelings don't help. As a matter of fact, they do the opposite."

Her unspoken words—*they hurt*—seemed to hit him like a punch. She saw a flare of pain in his eyes.

"Jake—"

"I *get* it, Amy!"

Doors opened. Fourth floor.

"If we could just be friends . . ."

He jammed his hands in the pockets of his jeans. "Yeah, feelings just get in the way, don't they," he said. "So let's just kick them aside. Go ahead, find someone less . . . *demanding*. Like Mr. Smooth."

He meant Ian, of course. She was about to protest, but the doors opened again. It gave her time to think. Ian? Jake was *jealous*.

Maybe this way is best, she thought. *This way, he'll stay away.*

The doors opened on the second floor.

Two of Pierce's thugs stood in the hallway.

For a moment time hung suspended as they faced each other, equally surprised.

Then they exploded into movement. Amy dove for the DOOR CLOSE button. The goons leaped forward.

The door began to close as one of them pounced. He wedged half in, half out. His face was mashed against the door as Amy kept hitting the button.

Jake sprang off the back wall of the elevator, slamming his foot squarely in the man's midsection. A split second later Amy followed with a hard chop to his windpipe. Jake shoved, and he fell back onto the carpeted hallway. The doors slid shut, and the elevator dropped.

"They'll take the stairs," Jake said.

Amy was frantically texting Dan.

THEY ARE HERE GET OUT NOW.

When the doors opened, she and Jake blasted through them onto the mezzanine. Farther down the hall, they could see the doorway to the emergency stairs. It opened, and the two men burst out.

Amy and Jake raced across the wide floor of the mezzanine. A tour group had stopped near the restaurant, their luggage piled around them. Amy leaped over the pile, and Jake followed. She risked a glance down at the lobby and saw Dan check his phone. He looked up at them, then at the exit. But he and the others didn't move.

There could be only one reason. They were surrounded.

She flew down the wide staircase, then leaped over the banister several feet from the bottom.

"They're outside, too," Dan said.

"Side entrance," Amy said.

The group weaved through the crowded lobby and sprinted through the side entrance. They jogged down Euston Road. Behind them, the men exited the hotel door and they saw them walking quickly, keeping them all in sight. There were six of them.

"What should we do?" Dan muttered.

"Stay on Euston for now," Amy said. "It's crowded. They don't want to make a scene."

"I've got an idea," Jake said. "We're near the British Library. We might be able to lose them there. Then we can double back to the Tube station."

"Worth a try," Ian agreed.

"With you, my man," Jonah said.

Pony was puffing hard. "I hope it has benches."

With a chilling sense of dread, Amy recognized the man who almost threw her off the bridge. She remembered the strength of his hands, like iron manacles on her wrists, being up against a wall of power she couldn't fight.

The plaza in front of the library was full of students with backpacks. It was easy to blend into the crowd.

They hurried past a tall sculpture and toward the front doors. Amy sneaked a look over her shoulder. To her dismay, she saw the six men fanning out across the plaza.

They moved inside the building. The reception hall was five stories high and crowded with people milling in the exhibition area, or standing near the information desk. A group huddled around a teacher lecturing about the architecture of the building.

"There are three exits," Dan said. "There's a guy at each of them."

"Three of them moving through the crowd," Ian said.

"Let's try this," Jake said. "I'll use my father's credentials to get us on a private tour. Then we can look for an employee's exit. There's always a separate exit."

"I'll go with you," Ian said. "My father donated some rare Indian manuscripts to the library. I might have some pull, too."

They all stepped up to the desk and Jake leaned over to talk to the young man behind it. Amy shot a look over her shoulder. She looked straight into the eyes of the man who threw her off the bridge. He smiled.

"Dan." Her voice was breathless. "We have to . . ."

"I saw him. Relax," Dan murmured to her as he and Amy tried to draw the man away from the others. "What can he do to us? We're in a public place."

"Just ask Sammy Mourad," Amy said. "We can't let them get too close to Atticus."

She had lost sight of the man. Her eyes scanned the crowd. Suddenly, she felt something against her back. A hand closed around the back of her neck.

"Hypodermic needle," the man said.

Her eyes widened. Dan froze.

"That's right, little buddy. I've got a needle right at sissy's spine. And when I plunge it, she's going to lose her legs. She's going to lose her speech. She's gonna fall, okay? And right by the doors I've got three EMT guys. Well, they're gonna *look* like EMTs in a sec. They're gonna take sissy here out on a stretcher. You're gonna come along, because you care about her, right?"

"Or else I'm going to scream right now," Dan said.

"Yeah? Well, then sissy gets *two* injections. And that won't be pretty. Got it?"

Dan said nothing. His eyes were full of fury.

"I *said*, do I have your cooperation? Good. And then all your little pals will follow, and we'll all go to some nice secluded spot." The hand on her neck tightened. "We can finish what we started, sissy."

Jake and Atticus were still at the desk with Ian. Amy saw a blur of movement. A long overcoat flapping as a boy with a ponytail moved away. It was just at the edge of her vision. A hand reaching into an interior pocket . . .

The man holding her was wearing an earpiece. No doubt he was waiting to hear that the other men were in place. Amy knew that if she moved, he would jab her. She could see that Dan was in the middle of desperate strategizing. His gaze darted around the lobby.

"Keep thinking, buddy. It's not gonna get you anywhere, but it's fun to watch your little brain on the move." The man chortled.

Pony put down two small items on the floor. Amy couldn't tell what he was doing. She could see fear on his face, but determination, too.

A beat burst out from the speakers. *DadaDAdadada, dadaDAdadadada, DAdaDA* . . .

Pony held one arm out, then the other. Then he jerked to the side. He was perfectly in time to the beat. Then he jerked to the other side.

He bobbed his head.

He took one step forward.

The infectious beat pounded. It was a worldwide hit, Jonah Wizard's "Make Me Happy or Else I'll Be Sad." People began to turn.

He took one step back.

He did the robot.

Amy widened her eyes at Dan. She knew the dance. Half the population of the *world* must have known the dance. Jonah's video had gone viral.

A small space had cleared around Pony. And suddenly the crowd was parting, and Jonah Wizard was sliding toward Pony across the polished floor on his knees. It was a trademark Wizard move.

The people standing nearby who could see burst into applause. Girls squealed. Boys shouted. Jonah jumped up and began to dance next to Pony.

"JONAH WIZARD!" someone screamed.

Dan stepped forward. He flung one arm out, then the other.

He took another step forward.

He took one step back.

He did the robot.

"What the . . ." the thug behind Amy muttered.

"Is this being filmed?" a girl asked.

Amy searched the crowd for Jake. He had stopped and was watching Dan and Pony, his face creased in a frown.

Oh, no. He doesn't know the dance. He's not hip enough.

He's just . . . Jake. He can name every Mozart opera, but he doesn't know hip-hop.

Jake thrust out a hip. He waved an arm.

The crowd moved back.

Jake was awesome.

Atticus joined him. The two were perfectly in sync as Jonah's voice boomed out.

Sad in my heart, oh it feels like a BROOM

Sweeps all the fly right out of my ROOM . . .

"IT'S A FLASH MOB!" Amy yelled, and the room erupted.

The hall went wild. Everyone in the lobby stamped to the beat and sang with one voice. They danced, laughing and singing, shouting the lyrics. The song had been a megahit, and everyone in the hall knew the video. Whether they loved the song or not didn't matter — it had been a global earworm. They knew the lyrics, and they knew the dance.

"We wait," the man behind her said, and she knew he was talking into his headpiece.

Amy dared to wave an arm. A young man next to her smiled and took her hand and yanked her away. She flew forward, straight into the surging mob. She was now part of the crowd, mimicking the movements, shouting the words. She tried to maneuver toward Dan and the others.

'Cause all I want is happy-ness

Don't you give me your depress,

Make my day, just acquiesce . . .

It was time to go, while the place was still jumping. Pony was wild-eyed, locked in a dance with a young blond student. Amy signaled to him, and he bent to pick up his gear. Jonah winked at her and followed. Jake and Atticus and Ian began to dance toward the doors, Ian stiff but trying, and Jake with surprising grace.

I never knew he could dance. . . .

She saw over the bobbing heads that the goons were scanning the waving, dancing, singing crowd, furious that she had escaped. She saw the others, now dressed in dark green EMT gear. They were trying to move through the surging, dancing crowd. One of the men got smacked by a waving hand.

Still mimicking the dance, they snaked their way to the front. As the crowd collapsed into cheers, they ran.

CHAPTER 30

It had never happened before. Never, ever, ever. Nobody had ever done it and many had tried.

Impossible. April May stared at her computer screen. She had just spent the last two hours running checks and counterchecks and rerunning them, and she kept coming to the same conclusion. She had to face the fact that just because she *thought* something was impossible didn't mean it *was*.

April May had been hacked.

Not only hacked, but *beautifully* hacked. Such an elegant, simple program. If she didn't feel like taking her computer and smashing it over Supreme Coder's head, she'd buy him a Red Bull and hire him. Or her.

The *beauty* of it—the hacker had set up a completely false system. A Trojan horse, if you will—and wasn't *that* an apt analogy, considering the Cahills' next destination—that had mimicked the real system enough so that she had spent all her time monitoring it. And *then*, if she used fake information, the hacker trailed her *back* to her system. Which had firewalls and alerts and alarms, but he or she had managed to break in long enough to *maybe* discover some information that April May was not altogether happy about.

Like, for instance, that WALDO had access to the CCTV feeds in major European capitals.

It had been a stroke of luck that she'd been able to pass on the information that Amy and Dan were in King's Cross station. She'd been able to hand off the information to J. Rutherford Pierce, which kept her demanding client happy for a nanosecond before he started breathing down her neck again.

Her e-mail alert chimed. April clicked on it. Another e-mail from Pierce, this one only three sentences:

```
Cahills on the move again. Last seen
at British Library. FIND THEM OR YOU'RE
FIRED.
```

What was it with this guy and threats? He lived for them. April fired back a reply.

```
Istanbul.
```

April felt anger and resentment swamp her, two emotions she did not allow in life or work. She sat quietly, letting them build and crash and then recede. She pictured a breaking wave, then a tranquil sea. J. Rutherford Pierce had a way of tap-dancing on her last nerve.

The Cahill kids had been discovered in the west of Ireland. She'd researched news accounts. No paparazzi had appeared to photograph the Cahill crazies doing something risky. No pictures at all, or mentions. Wasn't that why Pierce wanted to locate them? So he could deliver one of his "scoops"?

But while she'd searched she'd come across a random shooting off the Cliffs of Moher. A young woman had been out boating when suddenly, a bullet had slammed into the dashboard of her vessel. The boat had sunk and she'd been rescued by a Jet Ski. Some fishermen had complained about two boats racing through a harbor. . . .

April leaned forward and clicked through on her CCTV feeds. Multiple windows appeared, and she was able to follow each one carefully. When she found what she was looking for, she froze it. She zoomed in.

There were no paparazzi at the British Library. There was one heavily muscled man, and there was a glint of silver in his cupped hand. He was holding Amy Cahill's neck with one hand, shielding the move from the crowd. And what was that glint of silver . . .

A hypodermic.

She zoomed in on the faces of Amy and Dan Cahill. Fear. Desperation. Anger. All there to see in the taut muscles of their faces, their widened eyes.

She let the tape roll. And look, how Dan and Amy keep eye contact throughout. Look, how Dan was on the balls of his feet, ready to attack this muscleman.

These two were closer than close. Dan was ready to die for her.

The strains of Jonah Wizard's hit began. April's mouth twitched. She watched the flash mob form. She watched the joy and movement, but her eyes stayed on Dan and Amy and . . . oh, there they were, their friends. She isolated and clicked until they, too, were loaded into her software.

The e-mail dinged again.

```
Istanbul? Find out why.
```

"Not in my job description," April said aloud. She hesitated, fingers over the keys. She was beginning to realize that this job wasn't what it appeared. Her client was lying to her. Why? What did he want?

Was he trying to *kill* Amy and Dan Cahill?

A sick feeling grew inside her. April sat quietly, replaying the CCTV tape over and over. The silver hypodermic. The muscled thugs moving through the crowd.

April felt very cold. She discovered that she was trembling.

"Not in my job description," she whispered.

Was Pierce involved in this? Did he know?

She had to find out. Which meant she might have to break precedent and do something she'd never done before: fieldwork.

CHAPTER 31

Somewhere over the Mediterranean Sea

With a sack of cheeseburgers and some soft drinks in hand, they had piled onto Jonah's plane. They had eaten, napped, and now they were an hour from Istanbul and ready to hear about Troy.

"I don't get it," Dan said, peeking at Atticus's notes. "What's legend, and what's fact? This guy Paris falls in love with Helen and steals her away from her husband and takes her to Troy. So everybody gets really mad and there's a war. Like, for ten years. Agamemnon is Helen's brother-in-law so he gets up into Paris's grille and camps out in this major siege. There's a bunch of battles — heroes like Achilles and Ajax bite the big one. Even Paris dies, and he started the whole thing. Finally the Greeks get impatient and pretend to give up. They give the Trojans a gigantic wooden horse as a good-bye present, like — whoa, dudes, here ya go, we're going home. Except they hide inside it and while the Trojans are partying they jump out and start a battle and this time, they win the war. Except basically everybody cool is dead, so what do they get anyway?"

"That's the shortest summary of Homer's *Iliad* I've ever heard," Atticus said admiringly.

"And a great summary of most wars," Jake remarked. "What do they get anyway?"

"V cool," Jonah put in, nodding. He lounged back in the leather armchair, his eyes half closed. He had flown from California to Boston to London and now was almost to Istanbul. He was used to touring, but the Cahill schedule was worse.

"V cool, indeed," Pony said. He'd practically repeated every utterance of Jonah's since they boarded.

"Then some guy in the 1870s decides that Troy wasn't legend, it was real, and he starts digging," Dan went on.

"Frank Calvert," Atticus said. "But Heinrich Schliemann usually gets the credit, even though he had no real archaeological training and kind of messed things up. But he *did* find that Troy actually existed. So now we know that it did. There are seven levels, I think—"

"Actually, nine," Jake said. "Each of them comes from a different historical period. So for our purposes, the most recent would be the one at the top—level nine. Troy was part of the Roman Empire then. It had an aqueduct and water system, public baths, a central market, theater—quite an impressive civilization."

"So how could it just . . . die?" Ian asked. "How could

all of the cities die? What did the people do wrong?"

"There's lots of reasons," Jake said. "Sometimes it's a natural disaster that they just don't recover from. Or a dictator who bankrupts the treasury and starves his people. Or starts a series of wars that never end until the civilization is destroyed. It can be a combination of factors, too. Any civilization is vulnerable, no matter how mighty." He nodded at Atticus. "Atticus and I have been brought up with dead civilizations. We're used to taking the long view."

"But it's not like it could happen now," Amy said. "I mean, here we are traveling from one great city to another. Cities full of taxis and theaters and restaurants and museums and people . . . it couldn't all just go away. America couldn't just go away."

"Read the papers lately?" Jake asked. "Nuclear weapons, climate change, unstable governments . . ."

"One person," Amy said. "One dictator with enough power making the wrong decisions . . ."

"Creating an army that is indestructible," Ian put in.

"Could change the world," Atticus said.

They fell silent. There was one name in each of their minds.

Pierce.

When the plane landed and they were taxiing to the terminal, Dan spoke up.

"At the risk of being a total buzzkill," he said, "I have to ask. Do we have a plan?"

"I've been researching leopards," Jake said. "They're tremendous athletes. They can run up to thirty-six miles per hour and leap twenty feet forward in a single bound. They can jump ten feet up. They stash food high in trees. They can drag a hundred pounds or more. They hunt at night and have keen vision and hearing. They stalk their prey, then swat it silly and kill it with a bite to the throat."

"Wow, thanks, Jake," Dan said. "Something to look forward to."

Jake grinned. "With any luck you won't get that close, Dan-o. Anatolian leopards have been extinct for almost forty years. They once prowled the forests and hills of the Aegean and the Mediterranean. They were revered by the Etruscans and hunted by the Romans. Hunted by everyone, actually. That's why they're extinct."

Amy was looking at a picture of a leopard on her phone. "That's so sad. They're so beautiful."

"The last official sighting—they think—was in 1974. But I read a couple of accounts online from people who swore they saw one. A wildlife organization has set up some camera traps in the mountains—a constantly running camera, hoping to catch sight of something."

Pony reached for his computer. "What's the name of the group?"

"The International Wildlife Preservation Association," Jake said. "IWPA."

"There's something else," Amy said. "There's a small museum in southwestern Turkey—on the way to the mountains—that has a stuffed leopard. We've sent e-mails to the address but they haven't responded. They're only open on weekends. Sketchy, but definitely worth checking out. We just have to hope that if there is a leopard, it still has its whiskers."

"There's a ton of folklore about leopard whiskers," Jake said. "They're supposed to have healing properties, or even magical properties."

"So we find an extinct leopard, shoot him with a paralyzing drug, and pluck some whiskers," Dan said. "No problem."

"You only need six," Jake said.

"Well, in that case," Dan said, "piece of cake."

Pony looked up. "I got in. Usually these kind of do-good organizations just don't have the firewall protection they should. Because, let's face it, why should they spend the bucks to hire someone like me? So it's all crufty—it looks complicated, but it's stupid. Gritch, gritch, I know."

"Is he speaking English?" Atticus asked Dan.

"No, he's speaking hacker," Jonah answered, stretching and yawning. "The dude is awesome. Just listen."

Pony flushed with pleasure. "I bet this frogger flakes out on a regular basis," he said. "It's so totally barfed out. Anyway, here's my point. I hacked into their camera trap feed. Mostly a bunch of animals hopping by, right? But they also have an internal comments section on the feed. I snarfed up the file, did a quick word search program, and turns out there was a recent sighting that some dudes think is a leopard and some think is just a lynx, so some other wildlife dude went up personally to this spot and snapped a pretty clear paw print, but they're all 'we can't release this info yet' and so . . ." Pony turned his laptop around. A photo was blown up on the screen, a clear paw print in the dirt. "There's your leopard."

CHAPTER 32

Wilmington, Delaware

Trilon Laboratories

AUTHORIZED PERSONNEL ONLY

"Well, that depends on what you mean by *authorized*," Nellie muttered at the sign. She held binoculars up to her face. "It's hard to keep Nellie Gomez out if she wants in."

She just hadn't figured out how yet.

She had driven all the way south on the New Jersey

Turnpike to the final exit, the Delaware Memorial Bridge. She'd gotten lost three times trying to find the lab, and each time she'd ended up in Pennsylvania. Delaware was a mighty small state.

From across the street in a mini-mart parking lot, she had a pretty clear view into the lab's huge parking lot. The long, low building climbed a slight rise behind it. Weak sunlight glanced off the car roofs.

The parking lot wasn't very crowded. Most of the employees had been fired, according to Pony. She'd seen a caravan of black SUVs enter just an hour before. Men and women in suits had exited the cars and walked briskly into the building.

There was a guard booth at the entrance and a chain-link fence. Surveillance cameras every few feet. Bright lights would illuminate the parking lot at night. She saw it all, and she knew there was no way she was going over that fence without getting caught.

She'd have to find another way.

A young woman pulled into the mini-mart parking lot. She got out, adjusting the skirt of her dark gray suit. Her hair was pulled back into a tight ponytail. Her pumps had a moderate heel. She strode into the market and came out a minute later, sipping at an orange juice. She looked at her watch three times in the time it took to drink the juice. Then she tossed it in the trash and went back to her car.

Nellie recognized all the signs. The young woman

was killing time before a job interview. She watched as the job seeker got back in her car and drove a few hundred feet down the road. She turned into Trilon Laboratories. The guard leaned toward her, his hand out.

Driver's license, Nellie thought. *He's got a list. Checking it twice . . .*

Nellie tapped her finger on the steering wheel. What had Pony said? Pierce had fired everyone. So now they were hiring.

She knew nothing about pharmaceuticals or chemistry.

But why let that stop her?

Nellie pulled out her phone and sent a text to Ian. He had contacts everywhere and could set up fake references for her.

Within the next thirty minutes, she had run off a totally fabricated résumé at a copy shop. She was now Nadine Gormey, brilliant young chemist with a degree from MIT.

Within an hour, she'd dyed her hair back to its natural glossy black, scrubbed off her temporary tattoo, and bought a conservative navy suit. She had also purchased the ugliest pair of sensible pumps she'd ever had the misfortune to place on her feet.

Of course, the fact that she knew absolutely nothing about labs, chemistry, or pharmaceutical science might turn out to be a wee bit of a problem. But she knew that somewhere in a secret lab, Sammy was being forced to produce new experiments on the deadliest serum known to humanity.

In that long, low gray building, a horrifying future was beginning to take shape. She was going to expose it, or die trying.

CHAPTER 33

Istanbul, Turkey

Hamilton Holt walked quickly through the terminal at Ataturk Airport. His flight had been delayed, and he had only a few minutes to catch a cab to the private plane terminal. The airport was crowded with people jostling to retrieve their luggage, get food, grab coffee. Near the exit doors, men were milling, offering rides. Hamilton scanned them, looking for the most honest face.

Ride, sir? Ride, sir? Cleanest taxi in Turkey! Safe driver! Ride, sir? I am the cheapest! They crowded around him.

It was his face, Hamilton knew. His big, dumb, teenage American face. It was his sandy hair and his big grin. Everybody thought he was a mark, a backpacking teenager just ready to be taken advantage of. Usually, they were right. He was a Cahill, but he hadn't inherited much of the canny insights of a Lucian, or the charm of the Janus. He was Tomas, through and through. If you wanted to climb a mountain or scale a cliff, he was your guy. If you wanted him to open a door with a head butt, he could handle it. But you had to show him the door.

One of the men pressed in closer and grabbed his sleeve. "Need some wheels, dawg?"

Hamilton turned. Behind the sunglasses he saw his friend Jonah Wizard. "Dude!"

"Dawg!"

They bumped fists, then high-fived.

"What are you doing here?" Hamilton asked. "Nellie told me to meet you at the private terminal."

"We got in early. I've got the crew in a van, waiting for your esteemed presence. We're taking off for Antalya on the coast. Then we head for the mountains to track a leopard."

Hamilton was unphased. "Lead on, dude."

The rest of the drivers drifted away, knowing they'd lost a fare. Jonah steered Hamilton toward the doors. Neither of them noticed the muscular man in sunglasses and a black T-shirt who followed them outside.

Their driver, Adil, told them that the city of Antalya was part of what was called the "Turquoise Coast," and Dan knew why as he glimpsed shimmering blue-green sea and golden sand as they drove. Palm trees were fanned by a warm, light breeze, and they rolled down the windows to smell the sea.

Adil turned onto a wide divided street in Antalya. On one side, Dan could glimpse the curving turquoise bay and the glorious backdrop of the shadowy stacked peaks of the Taurus Mountains. They whizzed by palm trees and tourist vans just like theirs as they headed toward the harbor. In the evening light the bay was flushed with pink, and the sky was streaked with purple. People were out strolling, checking out the different café menus or simply sitting outside sipping coffee. Danger and leopards seemed very far away.

Why am I always arriving at places like this, and never really seeing them? Dan wondered. For once he'd like to go to an awesome place without looking over his shoulder. He'd like to travel the world again, this time without being chased or shot at.

If there's a world left once Pierce gets his hands on it.

When they'd asked Adil for the best place to find mountain guides who were both trustworthy and could keep their mouths shut, he had directed them to a coffee shop in Antalya and told them to ask for Sadik. They checked into the hotel overlooking the beach, which was crammed with happy tourists. Then they headed out.

The sun had set by the time they navigated their way to the old city, called the Kaleiçi, an area of twisting streets and alleys. They took several wrong turns, despite using the GPS on their phones. Finally, they located the alley.

There was no sign outside, but several tables were

out on the sidewalk, where people sat sipping coffee and eating pastries. The group pushed into the shop. Smoke curled in the air, and the buzz of conversation was energizing. The coffeehouse was mostly filled with men sitting at small tables, sipping black coffee out of delicate cups. There were several couches positioned facing each other, and glass-globed lamps in jewel-toned colors hung from the ceiling. Carpets hung on the wall, and mirrors reflected curling smoke.

They stopped for a moment as people turned to regard the newcomers, then turned back, and the buzz of conversation revived.

They sat at a table in the corner. "Do you think I can order a double-shot decaf grande no-whip mocha with a pump of hazelnut here?" Dan asked.

"Try it," Jake suggested. "I'd like to see how far you'd get kicked out the door."

They ordered coffee, which came several minutes later in small, elegantly patterned cups. The coffee was thick and dark, with foam floating on top. Glasses of water were also put on the table, along with a small bowl of sugar cubes.

Jake asked the waiter if Sadik was there. The waiter pointed to the opposite corner. A middle-aged man sat alone, occasionally taking a small sip of coffee. There was something daunting about him. He looked rougher than the urban, sophisticated men around them. He was wearing corduroy pants stuck into heavy boots and a white shirt, open at the neck.

"He looks like he could capture a leopard with one hand and pluck out the whiskers with his teeth," Dan whispered.

"Can you tell him that Adil sent us?" Jake asked.

The waiter headed over to the other table. He bent and spoke. The man flicked his gaze over to their table. He took a long moment to study them.

He made his way over, holding his coffee. He put the cup down precisely, then sat. "Adil told you about me?"

"He said you were a mountain guide," Jake said. "We need one to lead us through the Taurus Mountains. We're zoology students. We're looking for a leopard."

He shrugged. "There are no leopards anymore."

"We have reason to believe that there is one."

He shook his head. "Impossible. I have been all over those mountains and have never seen evidence of this. Just stories that evaporate into fairy tales."

"We don't think so. And we're willing to pay well for your time. We need someone to take us to a certain spot and let us see if we can track the leopard."

"If you are so sure you're right, hunting leopards is a dangerous game. What will you do if you see one?"

"Shoot it with a dart to paralyze it so we can photograph it."

He gazed at Jake with impassive brown eyes. "I see."

"We would pay double your rate."

He inclined his head to the side.

"With a fifty percent tip if we locate the leopard."

He took a sip of coffee.

"Can you get your hands on rifles with tranquilizer darts?" Jake asked.

"I make it my business to get my hands on anything if the price is right."

Jake waited. They all did. Dan took one sip of the strong coffee and it took all his will not to choke. He took a gulp of water, watching the man's face as he considered them. Dan tried to look mature and ready for anything.

"We will set off at dawn," Sadik said.

CHAPTER 34

Sadik showed up at the hotel in a battered Jeep. Now that it came time to part from Pony, Jonah, Atticus, and Jake, Amy felt uncertain. She realized that she hadn't been entirely honest with herself. She had taken a stand in Ireland and said she didn't need Jake. It had torn her up to say it, but she had done it. But now that she was here . . . she suddenly *needed* him desperately. She hated the feeling.

They said good-bye standing by the Jeep. "We'll text you as soon as we get into the museum," Jonah said. "So don't worry, homeys, we'll have your backs."

"I don't know about this," Jake said. "Maybe we shouldn't split up."

"You don't think we can handle a leopard?" Dan asked. "Have you taken a good look at Sadik? He's Darth Vader and Han Solo combined! Chances are we'll be together back at the hotel in a day or so."

"Right," Jake said, though he didn't seem to mean it one bit.

"Come on, Amy," Ian urged. He took her hand to help her into the van, and Jake turned away.

Amy faced forward as Sadik took off. She refused to look back. She didn't want to see Jake dwindling in the distance. She didn't want to cry.

Suddenly, the passenger door opened. A backpack thumped inside, followed by Jake, who swung himself into the seat, breathing hard. "Jonah and Atticus can handle the museum," he said. "I'm coming along." He met her eyes in the rearview mirror. "I think you can handle mountain climbing and a leopard. But maybe not both at once."

They stopped in a small village to pick up two friends of Sadik's, Orhan and Derin. The Taurus range loomed against a bright blue sky, snow still on the high peaks. Sadik took a mountain road that led around a series of switchbacks that had Amy clutching her seat. He pulled over in a small parking area in a high mountain pasture. They were the only car.

"If you want to find a leopard, we have to take the less-traveled path," he said. "Difficult climb."

"We can do it," Amy said, jumping out of the car.

Sadik led the way. The three guides didn't speak much. They walked ahead of the group, as sure-footed as goats on the trail. Amy and the others struggled on the loose rocks and sliding soil. It was hard to keep their footing. Only Hamilton was able to keep pace with the guides.

Climbing was exhausting. They made camp the first night and the guides spread out sleeping bags around a fire.

They were up at dawn, eating toasted bread, oranges, and a wonderful cheese Sadik called *beyaz peynir* for breakfast. The guides brewed the strong black coffee that Amy was now almost used to.

They set off, climbing steadily upward, pointing out the goats clambering over the rocks. The air was clear and cold, with snow patches dotting the landscape. The trees began to thin out, and conifers defined the landscape. They came across a field of snowdrops, and Amy began to feel she had ascended into a magical, mystical world.

"The mountains of Turkey are full of legends," Jake said. "You could say that the first beauty contest took place on Mount Ida. Paris had to choose the most beautiful goddess — Hera, Athena, or Aphrodite. Aphrodite told him that if he chose her, he could have the most beautiful mortal woman in the world as his wife. That was Helen."

"Ah," Amy said. "And so the Trojan War began."

"The gods watched the fall of Troy from Mount Ida," Jake went on. "You can feel the legends here. The history is in the stones and the ground. Even in the scent of the air. The same wild herbs grew here then. You can almost think we *can* find a leopard." He grinned.

"With the help of the gods, of course."

Jake's words revolved in her head as they climbed. She, too, felt something in the air that she couldn't define. For Jake, it was history and legend. For her, it was a presence lurking behind them. There were times she felt as though the leopard was tracking *them*.

She stumbled on the path, and Jake caught her. "Are you okay?" he asked.

She realized that she felt a bit dizzy, and her head ached. "I'm fine," she said.

Their guides spoke in low voices, and she caught them, too, looking over their shoulders.

They were close to the GPS coordinates now. Dan was struggling a bit and had to use his inhaler. They were in a rugged landscape of boulders and scrub. Above them were tall cliffs, rising like a wall in front of them. Odd shadows played on the surface.

"Caves," Sadik said. "The cliff is limestone. Porous rock. We could be standing on an underground river right now."

"Is there a way up?" Hamilton asked.

"There is a trail. But we need to make camp here. The trail is narrow and can be dangerous at dusk. Tomorrow."

Orhan said a few words in Turkish to Sadik and began to walk farther up the trail.

"Where is he going?" Jake asked.

"To scout for tomorrow," Sadik said. "Sometimes there can be rockslides that block the way."

They began to set up camp. Night was falling fast. Sadik went to an overlook and stood for a long time, looking out.

"Do you think someone else is out there?" Amy asked when he came back.

"There is always someone else out there," Sadik said. "We don't own the mountain." He squatted by the fire. "And then there are the things not seen. The spirits of the gods. The ghosts of leopards. Perhaps that is what you are chasing. A ghost who walks." He winked at her.

Amy felt a chill down her spine. Jake drifted closer. "He's teasing you," he said. "Don't let him spook you."

But she *was* spooked. She felt tired and drained, and when she pressed a hand to her forehead she realized it was warm. Probably from the fire.

It was close to dark now. Derin asked a question of Sadik. Sadik gestured up the path. Probably Derin was asking about Orhan.

Suddenly, they heard the noise of footsteps, rocks sliding down the hill. Orhan was moving fast, hurrying toward them. He said a word in Turkish.

"What did he say?" Dan asked.

Sadik ignored Dan. He listened intently to Orhan's rapid speech. He shook his head, but Orhan just spoke more insistently.

"What is it?" Jake asked.

Sadik turned to them. "A paw print. Orhan swears it is a leopard print. Not a lynx, not a jackal. A leopard."

"He is sure?"

"He is sure. We'll sleep with our rifles tonight. And you should have dart pistols as well. We should all be armed."

The museum turned out to be a private house that had been set up as the Museum of Historical and Ancient Curiosities. A faded sign read WELCOME TOURISTS! Another: KNOCK NEXT DOOR FOR CURATOR.

"This feels way sketchy to me," Jonah said.

"If Pony were here, he'd probably say it smells like bogosity," Atticus said. "Lucky he stayed in the hotel."

"High on the bogusmeter," Jonah agreed. "But here we are."

They walked next door to a small house and knocked sharply. After a few moments, a middle-aged man with lively eyes and dark hair streaked with silver opened the door. He was carrying a newspaper. "Can I help you?"

"We'd like to see the museum."

He burst into a wide smile. "Excellent! I shall fetch the key."

He disappeared for a moment and then reappeared. They walked back to the museum and he fitted the key into the lock. The door stuck, and he shoved it with a shoulder. "Excellent security, you see," he said. "The door sticks!" Chuckling, he led them inside and switched on the lights.

Inside, it did look like an actual museum. The walls were whitewashed and lined with cases. Atticus paused by a display of Roman artifacts.

"You know, some of the most interesting artifacts you can find are in these little museums," Atticus said.

"Exactly," the curator said. "This area is so rich in ancient cultures. You can't go for a walk without tripping over a Roman coin. Heh. And we have some fine pieces of amber that have preserved ancient insects. . . ."

"Fascinating," Atticus said.

"Bro," Jonah said, excitement in his voice, "I see our prey." He nodded to the very back of the museum. A diorama had been set up with an approximation of the landscape around them. A stuffed leopard was caught midstride.

"Yes, our Anatolian leopard," the curator said. "One of the last of its breed."

They approached. "I'm interested in taxidermy," Atticus said. "The eyes . . ."

"Glass. But they look like the eyes of the leopard, do they not? Green and piercing. Mystical . . ."

"The whiskers?" Jonah asked. "Are they real?"

"Plastic. So lifelike!"

Jonah and Atticus exchanged a glance. Defeated. They turned to go.

"We have a gift shop! Don't forget!" The curator hurried after them. "Lovely pieces of amber, replicas of Roman coins, lots of gifts to bring back!"

They kept on walking.

"And if you are interested in leopards—and who isn't, magnificent creatures!—I have some artifacts preserved in amber—leopard whiskers. . . ."

They stopped.

"You have leopard whiskers preserved in amber?" Atticus asked.

"Yes! In the ancient amber display, right . . ." The curator stopped. He reached out a finger. He pushed the front door of the display case. It swung open.

There was a short pause. Then he shouted, "Nooooo!"

"What's missing?" Atticus asked, but he already knew the answer.

"WHERE ARE MY LEOPARD WHISKERS?"

CHAPTER 35

Amy dreamed of Aphrodite and Athena, and of Olivia, snipping herbs, steeping them in spring water. Bathing her forehead. Placing a cool hand over her lips. The hand was . . . bigger and rougher than she expected.

Amy opened her eyes. Jake had his hand over her mouth.

"Something's going on," he whispered.

She struggled to rise. "What?"

"I heard noises. There are lights on the trail below. I think we've been found."

"What? Where are Sadik and the guides?"

"They took off," Dan said, coming up. "We have to hide. It's the guys that attacked us in New York and London. Six of them. I saw them through the infrared binoculars."

"But where will we go?" Amy asked.

"Only one direction," Hamilton said. "Up."

They quickly rolled up their bags. Amy felt as though she was moving through water. It was like a nightmare, except she was completely awake. She pulled on her fleece and her shoes and quickly followed Dan, Jake, Hamilton, and Ian as they made their way as quietly as they could up the path.

The path narrowed as they twisted and turned. The lights behind them moved relentlessly forward. Their breath clouded in the frosty air.

"They're moving fast," Dan said. "We could get trapped on the summit. I can see the headline now. CAHILL KIDS LOSE ALTITUDE FAST." She could hear the fear underneath the joking tone.

Hamilton looked up at the cliff face rising above them. "Think we can get up to those caves?"

"In the dark?" Dan looked up.

Suddenly, a bullet thudded into the dirt only inches from them. They all dove for the dirt and hugged it.

"Um, I can do it," Dan said. "For sure."

"They must have infrared scopes on the rifles," Hamilton said, training his binoculars down the mountain.

Another bullet thudded into a boulder nearby.

Hamilton fishtailed on his belly, crawling away. "Follow me!"

He brought them to safety behind a stand of boulders by the cliff as another bullet, then another, pinged into the dirt.

Hamilton looked up at the cliff. "Look, I think they're at the very end of their range. See the pattern of the bullets? They can't quite reach the cliff, I'm guessing."

"You're *guessing*?" Ian asked.

"They'll be in range soon, though. Our only chance is to scale that cliff now."

"And then what?" Jake asked.

"Hide in the caves. Hope help arrives."

"We're in the middle of nowhere!" Ian protested.

With another spray of rifle fire, they exchanged glances.

"Hamilton is right," Amy said. "We have to take our chances and climb."

"The cave openings are small," Jake said. "Let's stay as close together as we can, but there won't be a cave to fit all of us."

Amy pressed a hand to her head.

"Amy?" Jake looked at her, worried. "Are you okay?"

"Stop asking me that," she said sharply. "Of course I am." Her head ached, but she had bigger problems. She rose and faced the cliff. It was hard to concentrate. She felt dizzy, and she wasn't sure she could scale the cliff.

Behind her another bullet slammed into a rock.

I can scale the cliff.

She launched herself up and began to climb. Now that she was up close, she could see the rock was porous and offered handholds and footholds. There was just enough light from the half moon and sky full of stars to see, if she was careful. She forced herself to concentrate. *Think, Amy.*

She could see down the slope to the lights moving steadily upward. Dan was right behind her, Ian and

Jake below him, and Hamilton was scaling the wall next to her, the fastest of all of them.

Suddenly, a bullet slammed into the rock. Shards went flying.

"We're in range!" Hamilton shouted. "Hurry!"

She could see a cave opening a few feet above her. It was just big enough for her to climb into. "Dan!" she called. "Here!"

She swung inside just as another round of gunfire exploded on the cliff face. "DAN!"

She saw his white face only a few feet away. He was safely tucked into a cave. Hamilton was just above. Jake and Ian had found a cave big enough for both of them.

The cliff shone in the moonlight, serene. She texted the others.

REPORT IN. ALL OK? NO INJURIES?

One by one the reports arrived. Everyone was safe.

Amy settled herself in and faced out, watching the lights advance.

As the night wore on, the cold settled into Amy's bones. Sweat had dried on her skin, making her shiver. Her skin felt hot. She knew she was feverish.

Through bleary eyes she watched as the men slowly,

inexorably made their way up the mountain. They set up camp below the cliffs. They methodically set out sleeping bags and sat around a small fire. One of the men sat with a rifle across his knees, facing the cliffs. Once in a while he'd spray the cliff face, just for fun.

Her phone vibrated. She peeked at it. It was from Jake to all of them.

WAITING US OUT.

The men were waiting for daylight, Amy thought, resting her head against the stone. She licked her lips thirstily. How she wished she'd had a chance to bring water along. She rested her hot forehead against the cool stone of the cave wall.

Hamilton would put up a good fight. So would Jake. So would all of them. But she'd seen these guys in action. They had a Tomas boost, and it made them close to indestructible. She didn't think it would be a fight the Cahills could win.

She had brought them all here to this mountain. She had to get them out.

They were all separated by yards of cliff. If they ventured out, it would be easy to pick them off. Make it look like an accident somehow, the Cahill kids recklessly seeking thrills on a mountain and falling to their deaths with their friends.

She could see the headlines. She pressed her hands hard against her eyes. The pale moon reverberated in blackness behind her closed lids, light bleeding and bouncing . . . like fireworks in the fog, Amy thought, and wondered if she was delirious.

Then she heard a low, intense sound. Somewhere between a growl and a purr. The hairs on the back of her neck stood up. Fear caused her entire body to clench. Ears straining, she listened.

The growl came again.

It was behind her.

Amy flattened herself against the cave wall. She breathed in and out, trying to calm herself. She tried to think through the panic.

She couldn't leave the cave. The lookout would see her.

She couldn't sit here all night, waiting for the leopard to attack her, either.

It might not be a leopard. It could be . . . something not quite so lethal. Other animals growled like that, didn't they? *A lynx, a jackal*, Sadik had said.

Amy slipped the pistol with the paralyzing dart from her waistband.

Her eyes were accustomed to the darkness now. She moved carefully toward the rear of the cave. After a while, the ground slanted upward. The air felt close and smelled damp. She heard something . . . a *drip, drip, drip*. As she moved forward, she realized her feet were wet.

There was a stream in the cave. So that must come from somewhere. The ground was sloping more sharply upward now, and she struggled not to slip as she climbed. She kept walking, following the noise of the low, rattling sound.

Her nostrils twitched. Fresh air. She could smell it. There was another opening in the cave!

Amy soon began to see the faintest of light ahead. She had to drop to her knees, but she crawled out of the cave, right onto the summit of the mountain. The faint light was cast by the countless stars.

She heard the purring growl again. She froze. She could just make out a pile of boulders about twenty feet ahead. She gripped the dart pistol.

Suddenly, out of the darkness she saw a pair of gleaming green eyes. The shock of the sight and her shaking hands caused her to drop the pistol. She heard it skitter away, fall down the slippery shale, out into the darkness.

Terror paralyzed her. She had nowhere to go.

The growl came again, freezing her blood.

The green eyes reminded her of something. Her dream. Olivia had those eyes, green and clear. . . .

She thought at that moment of her ancestor. She thought of the courage and persistence she'd glimpsed in the pages of that journal. Of Madeleine, who had begun the Madrigals, who had also never given up.

And Grace. She thought of Grace. Her grandmother would stand, just as she was, facing that animal presence, and she wouldn't flinch.

She stared into the darkness where she knew the other presence was. The terror left her and she felt a sort of communion with the life that was standing only yards away under the trees, hunted, the last of its breed.

I need something from you. I won't harm you. But if you give me this gift, it will save my people, just as you would have wanted to save your own.

The darkness was beginning to lift. She could make out the edges of things. The tree trunks, the rocks, the leaves.

As the light grew and brightened, she looked behind to see that she was standing in front of a broad vista. Far below she could see men hurrying up the trail. They wore uniforms. So the guides had left them, but they had gone for help.

The men below were quickly assembling their gear. They were retreating.

Dan and the others were safe.

She turned back to where the leopard had been. Nothing was there. The light touched a flat rock and something gleamed. She walked forward.

Six whiskers.

She crouched. Were they real? She touched them with her finger. A substance clung to one of them, something caramel colored, a pretty shard of stone, and she brushed it away.

She turned as she heard the noise of tumbling shale. Suddenly, one of the thugs vaulted over the lip of the cliff. It was the short, powerfully built one with the blond buzz cut. He used the momentum of his leap to keep going, charging toward her.

Panic shot through Amy. She tried a flying kick. Her leg felt like lead. It glanced off his hard body as he took the last step toward her. He wrapped his meaty hands around her neck and squeezed. She could smell his sweat and see the determination in his gaze. But his eyes looked so dead. . . .

Black spots swam in front of her eyes. Her knees buckled.

The grimace of satisfaction on his face turned to an O of surprise. His eyes rolled back in his head, and he fell heavily to the ground.

Jake stood behind him, a paralyzer gun in his hand.

He dashed toward her. "Are you okay?"

Amy fell to her knees, gasping, and he crouched by her.

"Okay," she croaked. "Thanks."

His fingers touched her neck gently. "You'll have a bruise."

"Doesn't matter." She struggled to her feet.

"Amy, no! Wait . . ."

"I have . . . to show you." She stumbled toward the rock. "The leopard was here. She left me these." Amy held out the whiskers.

Jake walked over to the rock. "That's impossible."

"But the impossible can be possible." She weaved and fell against him. He caught her.

"I'm so dizzy. . . ." she said. She was happy to lean against him now.

"I think you have altitude sickness," Jake said. "I'm serious, Amy. We need to get you down the mountain."

"I saw her, Jake! I saw her eyes. . . ."

As the light grew, the confusion in her head was beginning to clear. "Over there," she said. She tried to judge the exact spot where she'd seen the leopard's green glowing eyes.

She walked past Jake, searching the ground. It was all rock and shale.

Except for one clear patch of dirt. She crouched down to examine it. It wasn't the impression of a leopard's paw. It was a boot.

ATTLEBORO CRIER

TROUBLE IN TUNIS

Dan Cahill a violent criminal!

By Luke Springer

TUNIS, TUNISIA – The latest on Amy and Dan Cahill's worldwide crime spree? Assault and battery. The law-abiding citizens of Tunis, Tunisia, on the Mediterranean coast, stood by in horror as the teen terrors launched themselves at a reporter. "The kid got him right in the nose!" says a bystander. "It bled like a faucet and ruined my new shoes!"

SEE PAGE 3